Before Kirk could hear if Kyle the *Copernicus* cracked open like a giant egg and pushed forth a massive bubble of plasma and white-hot energy. *Enterprise* was slammed back. She rolled away, creaking under the strain as support struts buckled and circuits sparked. The bridge lights dimmed and returned, but the ship continued to quake and rumble.

"Captain!" Chekov's voice. "Shockwave now pushing Isitri fleet—toward the colony!"

On the main viewscreen, the torrent of energy dissipated and the Isitri fleet could be seen rolling awkwardly toward the gas giant and its several moons, one of which held Berlis's colony.

Kirk didn't have time to consider the ramifications and instead was pounding at the comm. "Transporter room!"

"Internal communications are down, sir," Uhura said as she waved the remnants of a smoke plume from her console. "Trying auxiliary circuits."

"Sulu," Kirk barked around an intake of the acrid air, "take the conn." Two steps later, he was in the turbolift, zooming toward the transporter room. Long moments after that, he was facing Spock on the transporter platform. He motioned forward one of the security officers standing guard.

"Place Mister Spock under arrest."

STAR TREK®

TROUBLESOME MINDS

Dave
Galanter

Based upon *Star Trek*
created by Gene Roddenberry

POCKET BOOKS
New York   London   Toronto   Sydney

Pocket Books
A Division of Simon & Schuster, Inc.
1230 Avenue of the Americas
New York, NY 10020

This book is a work of fiction. Names, characters, places, and incidents either are products of the author's imagination or are used fictitiously. Any resemblance to actual events or locales or persons, living or dead, is entirely coincidental.

First Pocket Books paperback edition June 2009

POCKET and colophon are registered trademarks of Simon & Schuster, Inc.

For information about special discounts for bulk purchases, please contact Simon & Schuster Special Sales at 1-866-506-1949 or business@simonandschuster.com.

The Simon & Schuster Speakers Bureau can bring authors to your live event. For more information or to book an event, contact the Simon & Schuster Speakers Bureau at 1-866-248-3049 or visit our website at www.simonspeakers.com.

Cover art by Cliff Nielsen

Manufactured in the United States of America

10   9   8   7   6   5   4   3   2   1

ISBN 978-1-4391-0155-1
ISBN 978-1-4391-2345-4 (ebook)

To Josh,
for the language he taught me

"Loneliness is the first thing which God's eye named, not good."

—John Milton

ONE

"Tractor beam." Captain James T. Kirk spun toward his chief engineer.

Montgomery Scott turned from the engineering console and shook his head forbiddingly. "At this distance? Through that atmosphere? Impossible, sir."

"Their shields are failing." Spock was angled over his science station console viewer, its informative blue glow playing over his sharp features. "At the current rate of descent, their hull will be crushed in four minutes, sixteen-point-nine seconds."

"Mister Scott, set shields for atmospheric running." Kirk turned back toward the helm. "Sulu, close the distance. I want that ship pulled out of there."

"Aye, sir." Sulu's lithe fingers danced impressively

across his console. At navigation, Ensign Chekov answered Sulu's movements. Moments later, the navigator said, "In range, Captain."

Kirk kept his eyes on the main viewscreen. Tension made his shoulders knot up. First contact with a new warp-capable race was exhilarating, but the distress call dampened any enthusiasm and caused concern. "Spock?"

"Radiation from the gas giant prevents a detailed scan, but sensors indicate storm currents are pulling them deeper."

Sulu must have felt his captain's eyes on him because he began reporting the closing distance. "Forty thousand kilometers . . . thirty thousand . . ."

Scotty positioned his hands over the proper controls. "Almost."

"In range . . ." Sulu gazed deeply into his scanner. "Now!"

"Scotty—"

"Tractor beam engaged, sir."

Enterprise's tractors emitted blue energy beams that encased the alien vessel and pulled it slightly closer.

"Reverse course," Kirk ordered.

The engines struggled as *Enterprise* pulled the other ship through the tempestuous primordial gases. Kirk gripped the arms of his chair and seemed to transfer his will to the tractor beam to help tug the mass behind them.

On the main viewscreen, gas clouds eventually gave way to the dark vacuum of space. Kirk watched the starscape intently until the red lights on the helm began to flash. Chekov instantly checked his console, as the captain watched over his shoulder.

"Two vessels, incoming." Chekov looked back at Kirk expectantly but the captain flew out of his seat and toward the rail near the first officer's station.

"Spock?"

"Unknown design. Scanning energy signatures . . ." The Vulcan glanced up, making eye contact with Kirk. "They're charging weapons."

"Uhura, hailing frequency."

Slender brown fingers made well-practiced motions across the communication console. Uhura nodded quickly. "Open, sir."

"This is Captain James T. Kirk of the Federation *Starship Enterprise*. We are responding to a general distress call and engaged in rescue operations—"

Uhura removed her earpiece and instead read her console screen. "They're responding, sir—mathematically."

"Universal replies, Uhura." Kirk stepped up between his officers, but kept his eyes on the main viewscreen. "Spock?"

"Class eleven shields and weak disruptor cannons. And yet . . ." The first officer turned away from his scanner to impress upon Kirk the irony of the situation. "They appear to be warning us to leave."

"Don't they have sensors?" *If they did,* Kirk thought, *they were fools.* "We outgun them a hundred to one."

"Confirmed, Captain," Uhura said. "The message is a warning."

"Explain we're on a rescue mission."

Uhura checked the readouts on her board and shook her head. "I think they understand that, sir. Their message reads: 'Leave them to die.' "

"They're firing on the damaged ship," Spock reported.

Kirk ordered Scotty, "Extend our shields."

The chief engineer shook his head. "We'll lose the tractor beam, and they'll slip back into the atmosphere, sir."

"Another salvo, and the alien ship will lose cohesion," Spock said.

Kirk returned to his command chair and pounded the comm button. "Bridge to transporter room. Lock on alien vessel in tractor and beam all life-forms aboard."

As he watched the small vessel fade into the gas that surrounded the planet, Kirk wished he was at the transporter controls. He looked from the main screen to the speaker on the arm of the center seat and back again—until he saw a bright flare against the sweeping maelstrom of colors. The ship was gone. Kirk's jaw tightened until he heard Kyle's report from the transporter room: *"We have them, sir! Three individuals."*

A sigh rose in Kirk's throat but he wouldn't let it escape. Instead, he asked Spock, "The hostiles?"

"Breaking off, Captain. Retreating toward the inner star system."

Sulu's hands hovered on his console, ready to engage a course that Chekov had no doubt already plotted. "Pursuit, sir?"

"Negative. Continue scans and maintain red alert. Uhura, security to transporter room. Have medical standing by." Kirk hurried to the turbolift. "Spock, with me. Scotty, you have the conn."

"Jim, I don't think we'll need them." Doctor Leonard McCoy's tone was laced both with annoyance at the security team near the doorway and pity for the three unconscious souls in sickbay.

Familiar with McCoy's attitude and recognizing that the three aliens didn't pose much of a threat, Kirk sent the guards away. As they retreated out of sickbay, the captain got a closer look at the most colorfully dressed alien who appeared to be the leader.

Dressed in a medium-blue tunic and loose gray trousers, the being to whom McCoy attended was humanoid, slight of build with a bone-white complexion under a pinkish fuzz. He had no hair exactly, but the fuzz on his head was thicker and crest-shaped. He had large eyes that bulged even when closed, and flat nostrils without a pronounced nose—an interesting evolution.

A nurse removed a device from the being's wrist, and Kirk noticed that the even distribution of fuzz made it seem as if a pale child had been crossbred with a peach.

"How are they?" Kirk asked as McCoy scanned and reviewed the bio-bed monitor.

"Coming around, I think," the doctor grunted.

Before them, the peach man stirred, his bulbous eyes fluttering open. He was so delicate that Kirk wondered about his planet's gravity and makeup. Did his people, like the Vulcans, hide incredible strength in their slender forms?

The alien flailed his arms then pointed and gestured while looking pleadingly at McCoy and the nurse.

"Is he trying to speak? Is he injured?" Kirk came closer.

"He's *not* trying to speak," McCoy said, glancing at his Feinberg scanner. "No vocal cords."

"Captain, I believe he wishes to use the device taken from his wrist." Spock gestured toward the apparatus on the table to the left of the alien.

Kirk nodded and said, "Analysis."

The Vulcan scanned the device with his tricorder, then picked it up and inspected it closer. "A computerized communications device. No inherent threat."

Kirk made a gesture, ordering that the unit be returned to its owner. The alien sat up in bed, and relief flushed his pale countenance as Spock returned it to him. The alien placed the device on his wrist and began gesturing again. This time, however, a flood of tones emanated from the device.

The other two aliens began to stir. They looked panicked and unsure at first, but then, suddenly and perfectly synchronized, they grew calm and centered. Kirk found it curious, and filed away the thought for later consideration.

The universal translator began interpreting, replacing bleeps with words once the *Enterprise*'s computer learned the alien language.

"Can you understand us?" Kirk asked the alien who had come to first.

The peach man took in a breath, not quite a gasp. Kirk wondered if the reaction was the equivalent of a nod, but then the alien gestured at him. The translator took over: "Understand I. You make sound. Hear I and communicate."

Kirk nodded slowly and the alien mimicked the gesture as if attempting to duplicate a greeting.

"You who?" the alien asked, looking around the room and addressing the question to them all.

Kirk took a step forward and said, "James T. Kirk, captain of the *Starship Enterprise*, my first officer, Mister Spock, and Doctor Leonard McCoy. We responded to your distress call."

The alien looked from Kirk to the others—including his own people—then back to the *Enterprise* captain.

His slight features, which seemed even smaller in relation to his bulbous eyes, were excited and relieved. "I possess no knowledge of you, but you interesting very very. I called Berlis Aknista from Isitra Colony First. Excuse language barrier. We communicate thoughts. When travel space, device necessary for deliver information give you."

"Telepaths, Captain."

"Yes, thank you, Mister Spock."

"Do you have a written language?" Spock asked Berlis.

"Writing recent. No need past."

Spock nodded as if confirming a theory to himself.

"But you developed a manual language?" McCoy asked.

"Yes. Not all people think together. Some alone, single—disabled. They signs created—ideas communicate difficult but possible."

The syntax wasn't alarming to Kirk, though it was already improving thanks to the universal translator. There must have been something in the way Berlis was gesturing or the manner in which the device interpreted these gestures into tones that the translator still didn't understand. With time it would improve.

Kirk wasn't certain if he should avoid moving his hands when he spoke. He was concerned about gesturing in a manner Berlis and his people might find insulting, or that would accidentally convey the wrong thing, so he kept his arms at his sides and spoke as evenly as possible.

"Someone wanted you dead. Why?"

Berlis's face wrinkled with confusion as he said, "Why?"

"That's what we'd like to know. Why?"

Berlis and the other two aliens simultaneously looked at Kirk anxiously, as if the captain would be the one to soon supply them with an answer.

Could such naïveté be genuine? Kirk and Spock exchanged a glance, but the Vulcan offered only a curious expression.

Pushing out a breath, Kirk steeled his gaze. "Who attacked you?"

"Our people from Isitra Zero: homeworld."

Spock's eyebrow lifted in surprise at the information, and McCoy, even as he continued to scan one of Berlis's comrades, looked genuinely insulted on the aliens' behalf.

"And . . ." Kirk struggled to get the next question out, unsure of just how far he could go before seeming rude. "You don't know why they'd want you dead?"

"I know not," Berlis told him. "I Colony First leader I now return home from meeting with Zero council."

"Was there a disagreement at your meeting?" Spock asked. "Perhaps a heated one?"

Berlis made a quick synchronized movement with both hands. "No."

Kirk waited a long moment for Berlis to elaborate, but the alien said nothing more. Finally McCoy broke the silence.

"Jim, we should let them rest." The doctor gently pushed Berlis down against the bio-bed's pillow. "Their oxygen levels are still pretty low."

"Well, you're safe for now," Kirk assured the three aliens, and found himself nodding to Berlis. Then the captain smiled slightly, unexpectedly, and shared another brief glance with Spock.

Spock merely looked at the captain with interest. Kirk couldn't quash the feeling that there was something strange about Berlis. He did not think it was because of the nonverbal communication; it wasn't the first alien— or human—he'd met who used manual language.

After a second's hesitation, the captain nodded once more, and turned and left. Spock followed behind.

Once they were in McCoy's office, Kirk turned to his first officer. "Opinion, Mister Spock."

"While it seems unlikely that Mister Berlis would be unaware of the reasons his own people might wish him dead, he seems forthright."

His lips pursed into a thin line, Kirk grudgingly grunted in agreement but added, "There's something . . . odd about Berlis and his people. I can't put my finger on it."

"Perhaps your human intuition is at work," Spock gibed, as McCoy joined them.

"How lucky for you to not be burdened," the doctor said.

Kirk allowed himself a slight smirk that pulled up one corner of his mouth.

"Indeed," Spock replied.

"How long before we can talk to them again, Bones?"

The doctor's shoulders rolled in a lazy shrug, as he shook his head. "I'll let you know."

"As soon as Bones gives the word, move Berlis and his associates to quarters," Kirk told Spock. "I want you to talk with him again. Find out all you can—about their colony, the area, anything else that might help us figure out what's happening."

Spock, clasping his hands behind his back, nodded, saying, "Understood."

"Do we return Berlis to his colony," Kirk asked, "or hand him over to his homeworld's authorities? We choose the wrong answer, and our actions might cause a civil war."

"Agreed, Captain."

TWO

Two security guards flanked the entrance to the guest quarters that Berlis and his associates had been taken to. The close-knit group had requested a joint berth. Spock nodded at Lieutenant Sentell, who pushed the button that opened the cabin door.

The Vulcan stood outside until Berlis peered back and made a motion that obviously meant *come,* as the universal translator interpreted it. With his hands clasped behind his back, Spock entered just enough for the door to close behind him. "Am I disturbing you?"

Berlis huffed out two short breaths through slightly parted lips, which the universal translator interpreted as "No, no." The alien smoothed his hands over his fuzzy cheeks, apparently to make himself more presentable. *His preening,* Spock thought, *has an avian quality to it.*

"May I meet your associates?" Spock asked, stepping farther into the room.

Making a clipped gasp, Berlis indicated the sleeping area where both aliens were motionless, each in his own bunk. "They sleep," he told Spock by moving his head toward his own shoulder and closing his eyes a short moment. He sat in the chair in front of a small desk, and motioned for Spock to take a seat.

The Vulcan nodded once and moved smoothly to the available chair and sat down. "Captain Kirk wishes me to—"

"Questions, you have, questions?" Berlis asked. "We feel good. We try answer."

"We?" Spock glanced past Berlis at the two sleeping Isitri.

"They sleep. Exhausted—injury not habit. But good to answer questions." Berlis blinked at Spock expectantly.

Spock looked at Berlis's comrades and back at Berlis. "You're in contact with their minds right now?"

"Always," Berlis said.

"Are they aware of it?"

The short intake of breath was interpreted as "Yes." Berlis moved his head to one side, once again indicating the others. "We are always aware of one another."

"Interesting. Do you read their dreams?"

Berlis's eyes narrowed and his expression looked as humans might when they taste something sour. "Context strange," he said finally, after a long pause. "They tell me their desires. They do not write desires."

Of course, Spock thought, *a telepathic culture without books. They wouldn't understand the term* read *except in the context of reading something written.* "A dream," Spock explained, "is a series of thoughts or images that occur during a certain level of sleep in many sentient beings. Do Isitri experience dreams?"

Giving the question some thought, and seeming to test the notion, Berlis glanced back at his people and then at Spock again. "Not same you describe." He tilted his head to one side, indicating one of his associates. "Golo tells me he likes visit with wife when sleeps. Sometimes their children." He then tilted the other way. "Epiltan . . ." Berlis's face wrinkled into a strangely sweet smile. "Epiltan also likes visit Golo's wife." He chirped out a high-pitched laugh, then seemed to flush, as if embarrassed for the other man. "Epiltan," he said, by way of explanation, almost expecting that Spock would understand that it was simply Epiltan's way of being.

"Does Golo know Epiltan does this?"

"Of course," Berlis replied quickly, perhaps finding the question silly, but quickly recovering—realizing Spock couldn't know differently. "Golo and Epiltan . . . brothers. Their link strong very very."

Spock nodded slightly at the distinction. "So those related to each other have stronger telepathic connections."

Huff. Berlis's short outward breath told Spock he wasn't accurate. "They no relatives. Brothers." The illogical statement made Spock's eyebrow raise, and Berlis continued: "All normal link same. People choose communicate more deep with some, no others."

"Of course," Spock said. Berlis had used the term *brother,* or the translator had interpreted it, in the figurative sense, to describe not so much a familial bond as rather an emotional kinship.

"You different." Berlis stretched out his hand, pointing at Spock with the first and last fingers on his hand.

"Different from you?"

"No," came the short huff. "Different from others here. You think strong."

Spock lowered his head in acceptance. "Vulcans are telepaths. Usually there must be physical contact to . . . Are you attempting to probe my thoughts now?"

Berlis blushed again, his pale skin turning the same pinkish color as the fuzz that covered him. "Sorry I annoy—no intention—not realize action."

The probe of his mind had been so light, so peripheral, Spock believed Berlis was honest in his regret. It was likely that the Isitri merely had a passive telepathy that sought out nearby minds for communication and companionship. There was a similar connection among Vulcans, often unfelt and unnoticed. Spock had sensed the connection not long ago—when the Vulcan crew of the *U.S.S. Intrepid* had died in space. In fact, it wasn't the connection he'd felt even then, but the sudden severing of that link. Perhaps because he was away from most of his kind, Berlis was going through a similar withdrawal.

"I understand," Spock said. "No apology is necessary." Indeed, a connection to such a telepathy as Berlis's might be an interesting experience.

"I apologize continued," Berlis said. "Please, forgive, and let me answer your questions."

The briefing room tri-viewer showed a map of the current star system. When Spock flicked a button on his panel, the view highlighted a gray moon that orbited the same gas giant from which they'd pulled Berlis's ship.

"Isitra Colony First," Spock said. "The designation Berlis gives his home." He switched to an image of a green and blue Class-M planet closer to the Isitri star. "And Isitra Home Zero, where Berlis and his friends had been traveling, and the origin of the assault on their vessel."

Kirk glanced at McCoy, at his right, at Uhura, who was next to the doctor, and across the table at Scotty. When Spock spoke again, the captain gave his science officer his full attention.

"The purpose of Berlis's trip to Isitra, his first such voyage as colony leader, was to update his homeworld's council on the progress of Colony First, as well as to discuss ongoing negotiations with the inhabitants of the neighboring system." The viewer now showed a long-range scan of the next system. "On our charts, System Zeta Tau Nu. To the Isitri, the system of the Odib."

Spock described the Odib as a standard space-faring civilization, one with a spoken language and a conventional culture. This, apparently, had been a source of tension between the two races, and the Odib reportedly feared the Isitri.

"Why?" Kirk asked.

Spock shook his head. "Unknown."

"Speculate."

Spock drew in a slow breath and steepled his fingers, leaning back in contemplation. "Difficult to say without more information. Perhaps the Odib are particularly warlike. Certainly Berlis and his people are relatively peaceful."

"You mean the same people who tried to kill him?" McCoy asked pointedly.

Spock pursed his lips. "We don't have all the information regarding that event."

"And Berlis isn't forthcoming," Kirk said.

"He's been quite open, in fact." Spock's voice took on an almost excited tone, which was evident only in a slight increase in the speed of his speech. "He's given us a wealth of information about his culture. For example, the sign language they use has only recently been adapted with translation units for the purposes of space travel and negotiations with non-telepathic people. They have no books, no schools, no teachers, no mass communication, and while they have gestural languages, they have been developed for the few Isitri who lack telepathic ability because of illness or birth defects."

"But they never developed a spoken language?" Uhura asked.

"They lack a complex vocal apparatus," Spock replied. "A great number of Isitri are deaf. Spoken language would be of little use to them."

Kirk nodded, accepting the information, though it didn't help to explain why the Odib feared the Isitri. What would it be like to have negotiations with a race that communicated instantly with one another, discussing things covertly while in the presence of non-telepaths? It would seem secretive and the Odib would probably feel at a great disadvantage. Paranoia didn't often lead to peace.

"Their communication is fully telepathic?" Uhura asked. "Across the entire planet?"

"It is." Spock nodded once.

"Across space?" Scotty leaned in a little, his right hand motioning toward the now dark viewer. "Berlis's colony is on the tenth planet, and his homeworld is the fourth."

"Negative, the colony is not in telepathic contact with Isitra Zero. That is the reason for the colony—so that a group of Isitri can have different ideas, perhaps more inventive than the whole of Isitra Zero."

"Or perhaps more radical," Kirk said. "If the Isitri didn't care about the progress of their colony, or how Berlis was running it—"

"Berlis insists he does not run it," Spock said. "As I understand it, the Isitri share thoughts and ideas so freely that it's not possible for any one person to be in charge of any particular enterprise."

Kirk asked, "Then what's the purpose of a colony leader?"

Spock tilted his head and pursed his lips, indicating his answer was between educated guess and idle speculation. "Presumably to bring order to the chaos of a million individual minds all clamoring to be recognized."

Although he nodded as if his questions had been answered, Kirk still felt unsettled. What confused him most was a feeling he couldn't quite put his finger on. The captain turned to McCoy.

"Bones, what're the chances that Berlis and his people can make telepathic contact with us?"

"You mean send us their thoughts, or read our minds?" McCoy's brow crinkled in thought.

"Both. Either."

The doctor shrugged. "It wouldn't be unheard-of,

but since we need the universal translator to communicate, I doubt it. Physiologically, I haven't had time to study—"

Kirk turned to Spock again. "Have you sensed any attempt to contact you telepathically?"

"No deliberate attempt of which I'm aware."

McCoy could obviously read his captain's face well, and the doctor narrowed his eyes at Kirk. "Have you?"

Kirk smiled and shook his head. "No, no. At least I don't think so. Would I know?"

McCoy didn't quite grin and said, "If you heard voices in your head, you'd know."

His own slight smile fading, Kirk sat quietly a moment, looking down at the data card he was turning over and over in his right hand. He finally set down the card and looked squarely at the doctor. "There were certain questions I wanted to ask Berlis that kept . . . slipping away, while I was talking to him."

"In favor of what?" McCoy asked.

"Nothing. That's the point." Kirk shrugged. "I like him. I don't want to think negatively about him."

"What's wrong with that?" McCoy asked.

Kirk's eyes flicked up and saw from McCoy's reaction that he'd glared more intensely than intended. "I don't know him. How do you like someone you don't know?"

"Instinctive reaction?" Uhura offered. "We've all met someone we've taken an instant liking to."

The captain nodded and decided to change the subject. "Have we had any contact with the Isitri, Lieutenant?"

Uhura shook her head. "No, sir. And scans of communication traffic are extremely light, for reasons Mister Spock has now explained."

Kirk swiveled to face Spock. "We rescued someone the Isitri obviously didn't want rescued. What if we turn Berlis and his comrades over to them now?"

"Berlis doesn't know for certain, but suggests that doing so would be a death sentence." Spock's tone was overly forbidding, Kirk thought. Was there some emotion in it? Was Spock somehow outraged at the thought of it? Kirk was outraged, McCoy likely was, but Spock also seemed to be. It wouldn't be the first time Spock had allowed some emotion to lace his tone, but . . . maybe Kirk was projecting and saw something that was not necessarily there.

"Jim, we can't let this happen." McCoy pressed himself anxiously against the briefing room table.

"I'm forced to agree with the doctor," Spock said.

Kirk met both Scotty's and Uhura's respective gazes, each imploring him not to turn over Berlis and his comrades to the Isitri.

"I'd like to know the reason they've sentenced them to death," Kirk said.

"Indeed." Spock's coal-black eyes seemed to bore through Kirk. "No matter their reasons, whether perceived or real, would we hand them over for the Isitri to murder?"

Murder was an interesting word choice for Spock to make. Slowly, Kirk shook his head. "No."

"Captain, I strongly suggest we return Berlis, Epiltan, and Golo to their colony," Spock said. "It's the only moral choice we can make."

"The only one?" Kirk asked.

"Affirmative," Spock said tightly.

McCoy countered, "We could try to contact the Isitri and find out—"

"Inadvisable." Spock cut off the doctor. "First contact situations such as these are especially sensitive. Questioning their motives could be seen as overtly hostile."

Kirk couldn't really counter what Spock had said, but didn't recognize in it Spock's usual rational argument. It seemed almost as if Spock were reaching. Kirk wondered if the Vulcan was acting on gut instinct. Spock had spent the most time with Berlis and had a better understanding, if an incomplete one, of how the Isitri might react. But was there more behind his insistence?

The captain tested his theory: "We'll return Berlis to the Isitri."

Uhura and Scotty exchanged a concerned glance and McCoy nearly spoke but Spock reacted instantly—and irrationally.

"I cannot allow that," the Vulcan said tersely.

Kirk stared his first officer down. "You . . . cannot allow?"

"I . . . excuse me, Captain." And with that Spock rose and quickly left the briefing room.

"Security," Kirk said to Uhura and he and McCoy were instantly up and through the door. Across the corridor from the briefing room door, Spock was slumped against the wall, hands clasped tightly against his chest. He was breathing in and out so deeply that each breath lasted several seconds.

"Spock?" Kirk approached gingerly, then nodded for McCoy to examine the Vulcan. "Bones."

McCoy had no medical instruments with him and as the security men arrived, the doctor motioned them toward Spock. "Sickbay."

One arm held up to block the interference of the security guards, Spock seemed to instantly recover himself.

Nodding security off, Kirk stepped forward. "What happened?"

"My apologies, Captain," Spock said, his voice having regained its normal unaffected timbre, but his shoulders still tense with the effort.

"What happened?"

"Jim, let's get him to sickbay first."

Kirk nodded; if Spock was going to hesitate or object, he didn't show it. They went to sickbay.

After what seemed an interminable amount of time, McCoy finished scanning and nearly finished grumbling. "He's fine, as far as I can tell." He nodded to Nurse Chapel and she pressed a button on the exam table that tilted it forward, allowing Spock to step down.

The Vulcan went immediately to Kirk, who'd been waiting impatiently by McCoy's desk.

"I must sincerely apologize, Captain."

"What happened?" Kirk prodded. "Bones?"

"Physically? Nothing. Other than signs of mental stress."

Spock looked no worse for wear, Kirk thought, other than a slight slump of his shoulders. "From?"

McCoy handed Chapel a scanner and joined Spock and the captain. "I'm guessing there's something about Isitri telepathy that makes those perfect Vulcan brain waves a little less perfect."

"Inarticulately phrased, Doctor," Spock said, already sounding like his usual self, "but essentially correct."

Brow furrowing, Kirk felt his stomach tighten. Had Spock been victim of some telepathic attack? "They were trying to read your thoughts? Or communicate with you?"

"Both," Spock said. "And neither. I experienced a similar feeling when I first spoke to Berlis and—"

McCoy cut him off. "I thought you said he hadn't attempted to contact you telepathically?"

"I said no *deliberate* attempt was made," Spock corrected. "There is a passive telepathy I felt . . ."

"Maybe you and I did as well, Jim," McCoy offered, gesturing to include them both. "You said you felt something."

"Like an aura of good feeling." Kirk nodded. "It may be nothing."

"It may be something. And Spock, because of his Vulcan abilities, is more in tune with it."

"Apparently," Kirk said dryly.

"I have it under control now, Captain," Spock said.

Kirk looked to McCoy, who merely shrugged.

"Just the same," the captain said, "I think you should keep your distance from Berlis until he's gone."

"Jim, you're not really returning him to—"

Kirk cut him off. "The Isitri freighter headed for his colony."

Spock's left brow jutted toward his dark bangs.

A slight smile tugged at the captain's lips. "I won't lead him to his own execution. We'll return Berlis to his colony, and let the chips fall where they may."

McCoy nodded once, and Spock did as well, slowly, almost to himself.

THREE

The man had been on his ship a total of six hours, with half that time spent talking to Spock. And yet, even after his first officer's detailed report, and especially after learning that Spock was affected by the alien telepathy, Kirk was no closer to understanding the enigma that was Berlis of Isitra Colony First. As he and his comrades mounted the transporter platform, however, all his concerns seemed to melt away. Berlis's obvious innocence as he looked around the chamber in confusion was childlike, almost sweet. Kirk couldn't help but smile.

Berlis spun his arms, apparently asking Spock to explain what was happening. To Kirk's astonishment, Spock replied not verbally, but with fluid gestures.

When he was finished, Berlis, Epiltan, and Golo all looked satisfied and McCoy leaned toward Spock, his voice low. "You learned that in a few hours, Spock?"

"I did," Spock replied. "I've always had an affinity for languages."

"I thought that was music."

"They're much the same, Doctor. Even the manual language the Isitri use holds melody in its motions."

Kirk wondered if Spock had some telepathic help while learning the language, but then again, it *was* Spock. His mastery of alien cultures was what made him the best first officer in the fleet.

"Thank you, Captain Kirk," Berlis said, as Mister Kyle took him by the elbow and centered him properly on the transporter pad. "Because save lives, us, and return home, us."

Kirk couldn't help but return Berlis's infectious smile as Kyle returned to the transporter console and began pushing buttons. The captain glanced at Spock a moment, and wondered if he was blocking the same contagious smile from spreading across his face.

"Locked on to Isitri freighter, Captain."

"Energize."

Just as Kyle's hands moved toward the dematerialization sliders, the red alert lights began to flash. "Shields are up, sir," Kyle said.

The captain's fist snapping across the console like

a coiled snake attacking, Kirk punched the intercom.
"Kirk to bridge."

Uhura had been left the conn and the speaker crackled with her reply, *"Three incoming ships, Captain. We
believe Isitri. They're keeping their distance, but arming
weapons."*

"On my way."

"Come about, Mister Sulu," Uhura ordered.

"Coming about, aye." Sulu tapped expertly at his
console, and the stars swam across the viewscreen until
the three Isitri ships came into view.

"They're backing off," Palmer said from navigation.

Chekov was hunched over Spock's scanner console.
"They—two of the ships are powering down weapons
and engaging a course that will take them alongside the
freighter." Twisting slightly, the ensign looked to Uhura
with some confusion. "The third ship continues to
back off, and is maintaining weapons lock."

Uhura and Sulu exchanged a glance. "What're they
doing?" the helmsman asked, more to himself than to
anyone else.

When Kirk and Spock exited the turbolift, Uhura
relinquished the center seat to the captain and gave
him the latest status; Chekov returned to navigation
as Spock took back his console, and Palmer retreated
to the engineering station on the upper bridge. Ensign

Miller nodded to Uhura and took an auxiliary bridge station in case he was needed again.

Kirk lowered himself into the command chair. "Any hostility from the two Isitri ships that stood down, Mister Spock?"

"None." Spock looked over at the captain from his scanner. "And the third vessel is now turning back toward Isitra Zero."

It was anticlimactic, yet the bridge was still a block of tension. Kirk felt unnerved by a problem that seemed to require no further resolution. Why would three Isitri ships charge weapons only to have two of their number fall in sync with Berlis's freighter? Why would the other ship retreat, tail between its legs?

Turning toward Uhura, the captain ordered, "Try to hail the two that joined the freighter, Lieutenant."

"I have been, sir. No response."

Kirk got up and went toward the turbolift. "Maintain yellow alert. Uhura, you have the conn. Spock, let's talk to Berlis."

Berlis, Epiltan, and Golo were chatting with McCoy. When Kirk entered the transporter room again, he found all four laughing and Lieutenant Kyle smiling warmly. Isitri's laughter, perhaps because of the lack of vocal cords, had a decidedly chirpy quality to it, which added to the aliens' avian-like demeanor.

"Mister Berlis," Kirk said, "it would seem you're already aware that the crisis is averted."

"Yes," Berlis replied, his hand pointing to the red-alert light near the doorway. "Lights stop on, off. Only off now."

Kirk glanced up at the light and nodded. Of course, the lack of flashing lights made Berlis calm. The alien seemed to trust that he was safe on *Enterprise*. Somehow the notion also calmed Kirk—to know that his ship was safeguarding someone who needed protection.

The bosun's whistle sounded and the captain gestured for Kyle to activate the comm. "Kirk here."

"The Isitri colony freighter signals they're ready for transport."

"Thank you, Ensign. Kirk out."

Kyle held the transporter controls ready as Berlis and his crew mounted the platform again. This time, nothing stopped them from activating transport: the good-byes Berlis issued were final and the sparkle and hum of dematerialization whisked the Isitri away.

It wasn't until they were on the turbolift heading back to the bridge that Kirk first sensed a change in his own mood, and a side-glance to McCoy suggested the doctor was feeling the same. The feeling only came to fruition when silence fell between them once Kirk was sitting in the command chair. McCoy at the captain's left, they both watched the viewscreen as Berlis's Isitri ships disappeared into the distance.

Turning toward Spock's station, Kirk began to ask a question at least twice before finally calling the science officer over to the command chair.

"Captain?"

"Berlis's telepathy . . . I feel its absence. The warm feeling I had dissipated once he left. I felt . . . a loss. As if someone I cared about were going away and I would miss them."

McCoy looked away slightly. Spock merely offered silence.

His lips pressing into a thin line, Kirk could feel his annoyance ebbing. "Did you feel anything? At all? Either of you?"

When McCoy's eyebrow twitched and the doctor's lips pulled down into a slight frown, Kirk knew he was onto something. "You did."

"Well, maybe a little disappointment. I wouldn't call it a feeling really, just . . . uh . . ."

Kirk nodded and turned to Spock. "I don't suppose—"

"I'm quite sure I'd recognize a *feeling* if one had presented itself," Spock said dryly.

"I'm not," McCoy quipped.

"I assure you, Captain, my telepathic defenses are quite strong." Spock's voice lowered in tone, for the sake of his own privacy. "There have not been, nor will there be, any such incidents as before."

The captain believed him, but worried about his

Vulcan friend. "The question is how long must you keep your mental shields up? What's the range of their telepathy?"

Spock considered his answer for a brief moment. "Unknown. According to Berlis, the entire planet and colony respectively communicate, instantaneously, so at least planet-wide, but not far enough to traverse the star system."

"Somewhere in between," McCoy said.

"Obviously."

Kirk swiveled around toward port. "Palmer, how long before we have warp speed?"

The engineer turned from her station, crisply reporting, "Another twenty minutes or so, sir."

"Uhura, was there any contact with the Isitri ship that didn't join Berlis's freighter?"

Slightly turned away from her console, but always able to do several things at once, Uhura was coding some command into her board with one hand, and balancing her earpiece with the other. "No, sir. They refused to answer hails."

"It's possible that their communications officer was on one of the other two ships," Spock offered. "Berlis indicated that one communicator per expedition is not uncommon."

As Kirk watched the small dot on the main viewer shrink farther into the starscape, he searched for the feeling he'd had before—the sense of loss when Berlis left. It was gone, and now that it was, he wondered if it was ever really there.

"Mister Spock," he said finally, "I think it's time we made official first contact with Isitri Zero."

"Approaching the fourth planet, sir." Sulu looked back toward the command chair for a moment, then eyed Chekov's station to make sure he was in synch with the navigator.

Kirk watched the lush green planet as it grew closer on the viewscreen. "Uhura?"

"They're receiving us, Captain. Replying with an approach vector for orbit."

The captain nodded. "Transfer coordinates to the helm." He rose and moved toward the science station. "Spock?"

Gazing from his sensor cowl to a screen above him, Spock read the close-range scan results. "No natural satellites, but three orbiting platforms with life-forms aboard. Various other small orbital devices, seemingly monitoring the planet or scanning space."

Kirk looked back to the viewscreen regarding the planet. "Any hostility over our arrival?"

To be thorough, Spock doubled-checked. "None detected. There are several large cities across the two southern continents, any of which might hold defense systems or ships, but no evidence of active aggressive posture."

"Standard orbit, Mister Sulu." The captain returned to the command chair. "Uhura, transmit our intentions to make an official visit and—"

"Captain." Uhura turned fully toward Kirk, pulling out her earpiece but leaving it hovering near her earlobe. "They're asking to speak to *me.*"

Kirk leveled his gaze at Spock, who offered his opinion. "They might assume that the captain of the ship is also the communications officer."

"There is a certain logic to it," Uhura said with a playful smile.

His eye returning the twinkle he saw in hers, Kirk nodded at her. "Will you explain to them that I'll be substituting for you, if they'll permit me to visit?"

"Of course, sir."

Kirk pushed himself from the center seat and toward the lift. "Mister Spock, you have the conn."

The beam-down coordinates the Isitri had offered would leave Kirk and McCoy in the Main Council building at the center of Isitra Zero's capital. A bright room, vividly decorated in dazzling colors, materialized around them. With no one to greet them, they had time to take in the setting: artwork, clusters of seating thickly upholstered in shimmering fabrics, and at the center of each seating area, a small pool of water, neither deep enough nor big enough to accommodate anything but drinking or the washing of hands. Kirk wondered whether, given the Isitri's birdlike qualities, they were birdbaths.

An automatic door parted and a slight Isitri walked into the room, greeting both Kirk and McCoy with a smile and a strange hiss of breath. He—or she, since Kirk wasn't really sure how gender was differentiated among the Isitri—merely motioned for them to follow.

The doors opened to a corridor that they didn't walk down; instead, they turned directly into another room just meters from the doorway. Another larger set of doors opened to reveal a rather spare room with a round table made of what looked like stone but that also had the graininess of wood. As the Isitri who brought them in joined the others at the table—there were a total of seventeen—Kirk realized which seemed male and which female: like Berlis and his comrades, the males had pinkish fuzz covering them. The females had a slightly darker, almost lavender hue and somewhat thicker frame.

Two seats down from the man who'd led them in was a lavender Isitri. She stood and Kirk assumed she was the council leader.

Her arms moving swiftly, a translation unit began chirping on her wrist, and the universal translator quickly interpreted her meaning. "Hello. We are Isitri Council Zero. You are commander of the ship above? Why have you hindered our justice?" Either because this communicator was used to talking to off-worlders, or because his universal translator now had a better understanding of the language, her speech seemed tighter syntactically.

"I'm Captain James T. Kirk, representing the United Federation of Planets. I'm sorry that we interfered in an internal Isitri matter. That wasn't our intention, but we replied to a distress call and felt ethically bound to respond. Without knowing the crimes Mister Berlis may have been charged with, we—"

Suddenly a man across the room stood up and looked at Kirk but it was the woman who spoke and the timbre of the universal translator changed. Apparently the entire council would speak through her, and her tone would change depending for whom she was speaking. "Captain, Berlis is charged with no crime."

"But isn't he sentenced to death?" McCoy asked, unable to, much to Kirk's annoyance, keep his attitude out of the question.

"Yes," the Isitri man said through the woman. "For it is either he who shall die . . . or all of Home Zero."

FOUR

Since there was no real voice to echo off the Isitri Council chamber's walls, the universal translator's sterile intonation failed to capture the regret expressed on each of the seventeen Isitri faces before Kirk. Body language was more powerful than words, and a thick silence followed the Isitri man's declaration of why Berlis must die.

Yet there was still no concrete explanation—and Kirk needed more information. McCoy obviously did as well, and Kirk saw he was ready to say as much, so he jumped in before McCoy could. "Honored Isitri Council, our policy is not to knowingly involve ourselves in situations internal to your planet and politics, but having met

Berlis, you'll excuse me if I wonder exactly what threat he poses."

"We need not tell them."

"They won't understand."

"I believe they will."

"I believe you have the brain of a small domesticated animal."

Though all the statements came from the designated speaker, each one was delivered from several different sources. McCoy smiled at the last comment, and apparently embarrassed, the council discussed things more discreetly from that point on.

"I suppose we'll just think good thoughts to ourselves," Kirk muttered to McCoy; the woman interpreted Kirk with gestures, perhaps for the members of the council who couldn't hear. A collective chuckle rose from the members, and Kirk was positive he heard it cascade out of the room and down the hall. He wondered if it made its way across the city, and then the planet. Probably so. In a network of connected minds, new stories and humorous jokes were doubtless a commodity, and Kirk's irony was perhaps not lost on the entire race of Isitri.

"My niece likes you," one of the Isitri said.

Another added, "So does my brother."

"And my wife."

"And my domesticated animal."

Again, the group laughed, their nostrils opening

and closing, emitting their characteristic high-pitched chirp.

The man who seemed to be the most talkative among them stood and walked toward Kirk. "Captain, I must apologize for our less serious council member. He's often a problem." He glared at one of the members. "Understand that while we cannot read your thoughts, we consider ourselves good judges of character. I'd like to trust you."

This Isitri, Kirk noticed, was chunkier than Berlis and his two comrades. Kirk was unsure how much it had to do with the female interpreter, but this man spoke more elegantly. This council probably dealt with the Odib Spock had mentioned, and perhaps other races with whom the Isitri had come in contact. Although, a race of telepaths could conceivably appoint any individual or group as representative. The female interpreter explained that while Kirk stood here speaking to this group of seventeen, another group in another city listened and debated. For Kirk, it was a disconcerting notion: to be at odds with such a council, for example. How did one then convince an entire planet of one's position?

"Esteemed council member," Kirk began.

"My name is Chista," the man said via the interpreter, and then introduced the others. The fifteen names became a blur for Kirk. Interestingly, he did not introduce the interpreter.

"Chista, can you explain the specific reasons why Berlis must be killed?"

"It is not a decision we come to lightly, Captain, but one we must act on swiftly, especially now." Chista stopped pacing and, facing Kirk, drew in a short breath. "I am being told that I've begun this discussion too dramatically, and have not gotten to the point. Perhaps a more personal setting and more intimate conversation." He indicated a side door—which opened, perhaps on mental cue—and gestured for Kirk and McCoy to walk through. The female interpreter followed as well.

The room was certainly friendlier: soft seating and various shelves holding elaborate sculptures. While it suggested the warmth of a library, there were no books. As Spock had discovered, a culture that relied on telepathy in so absolute a manner had no need for them.

Chista sat and invited Kirk and McCoy to sit as well. The interpreter stood to the side of them, so she could do her job. Kirk had to remind himself to look at Chista, and not at the interpreter, since the one communicating was not the woman, but rather the Isitri man before them. He'd had enough experience to know that not facing the person whose words were being spoken was considered rude in many cultures.

"You have obviously talked with Berlis and enjoyed his company," Chista said. "There is much to admire in that young one. But unfortunately, there is also much to fear."

"He didn't seem dangerous," McCoy said. It was only the second thing he'd said since they'd beamed down, which was unusual for the doctor.

"My chief medical officer, Leonard McCoy."

"Medical Officer," Chista said, as if it were part of McCoy's name. "He is not physically a danger, but as all things Isitri, the problem is more mental."

Kirk and McCoy exchanged a glance, both recalling Spock's episode. What had happened wasn't dangerous, but it *was* unusual. Was Chista referring to similar incidents? They waited for him to explain but there was a long silence. The council man certainly seemed to have a sense of the dramatic, dropping hints frequently but never giving the full picture. Then again, he was likely having a planetwide conversation about what he should say. It was a wonder that anything ever got done on Isitra Zero. How would a Federation politician do anything with all his constituents in constant contact? *Actually*, Kirk thought, *such accountability might not be a bad thing*.

Eventually, Chista spoke again. There was probably some delay in this communications roundabout, as the Isitri conveyed his thoughts to the interpreter, who signed for her wrist device, which chirped to Kirk's universal translator. It was successful, if complicated. "We are a very open people, Captain, but many off-worlders don't understand that we are a large group of individuals. We are not a hive mind. There are those who believe I should not be confiding in you. Like the Odib, you could fear us, and wish to destroy us."

"That won't happen," Kirk told him.

The quick gasp that followed was Chista's acceptance of Kirk's claim. "Most of us believe that. Simply not all. But I have decided that your act to save Berlis shows us your character, and that of your people." His jaw quivered a little, and the interpreter remained silent. Kirk wondered if Chista was indulging in an Isitri sigh.

"We'd like to help if we can, Chista," Kirk said. "The Federation could mediate a dispute between you and Berlis, or—"

Chista made a short huff. "You misunderstand. We have no dispute. I must explain fully." The man's round belly sat on his lap like a package before him and he fidgeted uncomfortably beneath. "We begin communication with our young very early in their gestation. Soon after higher brain functions begin, so does our telepathy. Very simple at first, of course, as the brain is still growing and mapping pathways. We feel our children's emotions, and allow them to feel ours. This is something non-intimate adults do not do, except with close family members, as our emotions are one of the things that keeps us being individuals. As you can imagine, we bond to our young quite tightly and quite early, and when their telepathy grows, they reach out and touch the community as a whole."

"They speak," McCoy said, "before they're born."

In reply, Chista gave his Isitri nod: a slight inward breath. "Sometimes much to the chagrin of their parents," he said with a chirpy chuckle. Kirk saw his flat nostrils flare a little and realized the sound came from there.

Kirk and McCoy smiled. Aliens could be so different from humans, yet so similar in as many ways, including when it came to the frustrations of being a parent.

"Occasionally, a child has a telepathic ability that exceeds the strength of most Isitri. These children are undisciplined and have a tendency to push their thoughts and emotions on those around them. Usually, with training, this can be controlled. Every few generations there is a genetic mutation that produces what we call a 'troublesome mind.' Such a mind is not only uncontrollable, but also its telepathic aptitude is such that it can direct the minds of others."

"Berlis," Kirk said, a sour realization sinking in.

But Chista puffed out an opposing breath. "Berlis is the most troublesome mind of all, Captain, as his telepathy is the strength seen, thankfully, with great infrequency." The Isitri clasped his arms, seemingly chilled by the very thought of Berlis's power. "You must understand, we use our telepathy as a chain of vast communication that washes across the planet in waves and cross-waves. Berlis has the ability to not just influence the chain—he can control it."

Did that mean he was controlling Kirk on *Enterprise,* and Spock was trying to break the connection, or was Spock being controlled? Kirk wasn't sure. But he knew he needed to find out.

"He never received training to manage his ability?" McCoy asked.

"No," Chista said. "Had we known of a power as strong as his, his life would have been terminated in utero, as soon as the ability manifested." In reaction to McCoy's expression, Chista added: "In ancient times, the mother was killed as well. More recently, since the invention of space flight, in cases where the abnormality is not quite as strong, the person in question is exiled from her own kind."

"Berlis slipped through the cracks," Kirk said. The idiom was lost on the interpreter, and she asked him if he could rephrase the statement. "How did Berlis survive this long?"

"We don't know." Chista paused a moment, perhaps receiving information from the other Isitri. "We believe his ability must not have manifested until adulthood," Chista continued. "Since he was on Colony First, his growing control of others was not realized until he was elected to visit Isitra Zero. During his time with the council, he controlled us covertly—perhaps unknowingly—and we did not even realize it had happened until Berlis left the planet."

"Sir," McCoy began, and seemed unsure how to ask his question. Kirk was glad the doctor was being careful with his words. "Why wouldn't it be possible to train Berlis now as others have been?"

"His mind is too strong. And such training takes place on the preborn, not an adult mind that has been linked with so many others for so long." Chista must have seen that Kirk and McCoy didn't fully understand. "A troublesome mind must be isolated from most people. For any Isitri this is a difficult task, as we are so very intertwined with one another but for those as strong as Berlis . . ."

"You said he may not even be aware he is doing this. How can you sentence him to death if he doesn't know what he's done and isn't given a chance to stop?" Kirk asked.

"He cannot stop. No more than you could be asked to stop breathing. His nature is to destroy." Chista—or one of the other several billion Isitri—must have sensed Kirk was dissatisfied with that explanation. "Captain, this decision isn't made out of mere tradition. The risk is too great. Isitri history is riddled with such troublesome minds subjugating all for the span of a lifetime." Chista's jaw quivered and he sat back. He seemed to get lost in thought for a moment, then looked back to Kirk. "Ones weaker than Berlis have, in our past, usurped people's individuality for generations. Only upon their deaths would the entire planet come out of its mental slavery." He leaned closer now, his bulbous, yellow eyes sharp and focused. "Imagine it, Captain: As a young man you're suddenly under the total control of another mind. When that mind dies you have your life back. Except you're now an old man, and there *is* no life to live." The Isitri Council man let that thought sit a moment, then drew himself even closer. "Now multiply that tragedy . . . by a planet."

Kirk and McCoy exchanged a morose glance. *The ultimate dictatorship,* Kirk thought.

"Wouldn't it be possible to isolate Berlis, so he isn't a threat?" McCoy asked.

"We have tried such things, Medical Officer." Chista's expression was one of deep regret, or so it seemed to Kirk. With any alien race, however, Kirk realized he could be projecting; emotional facial expressions differed by culture. "Last time a troublesome mind ruled," Chista said, "his reign was twelve years. A war began with the Odib, because the mind in control believed them to be a threat to us. Millions died on both worlds, before the Odib finally managed to destroy the city where the mind lived." His jaw was quivering again, and Kirk was now certain the quiver was the equivalent of sighing. "The Isitri people woke from their sleep," he continued, "to find their children dead, their cities in ruins, and the Odib vowing that the next time we lost control to such a ruler . . . would be the last."

"I understand." Kirk felt his throat tighten around the words. He *did* understand, and the notion was horrifying.

"Our people, and peace with Odib, depends on Berlis's death, Captain," Chista lamented. "Do you not owe us your assistance? But for your interference, he would already be dead, and the threat of war averted."

The only thoughts Kirk could muster would speak to duty and good intentions . . . but it all seemed hollow since his actions *had* put billions in harm's way. "What kind of assistance?" Kirk finally asked, and avoided looking at McCoy.

Chista was eager to make his case. "Should we send a covert assassin, they would fail, because an Isitri mind would be instantly recognized and compromised. One of *your* people, however . . . that mind would not be recognized."

"No," Kirk said, shaking his head. "We can't carry out an execution for you."

Chista pushed out a series of quick, powerful breaths. "If Berlis had been left to die, we wouldn't be on the verge of war. The blood of millions will be on your hands, Captain."

"What war?" McCoy demanded, obviously as distraught as Kirk was over the situation.

"If Berlis returns to Isitra and reads the plan in our

minds to end him, we will all be under his control for certain. And the Odib will destroy us."

"But why?" McCoy demanded.

Kirk answered for Chista: "There's a peace treaty they must have signed. If one of these troublesome minds develops, and the Isitri don't take care of the situation, the Odib will." The Isitri gasped, acknowledging that Kirk was correct.

"Odib Ambassador Sa-Gahnesaam is, at this moment, in the southern capital," Chista admitted. "He demands the council provide proof that the troublesome mind we're bound by law to reveal to the Odib . . . has been destroyed." Lowering his head to one side in what appeared to be an expression of sadness and exhaustion, Chista sank back into his seat. "If you do not end Berlis for us . . . millions, perhaps billions, will die."

FIVE

The Isitri Council needed to deliberate with the sister council that had been conversing with the Odib ambassador. Kirk and McCoy were offered a brief tour of the area, and the interpreter served as their guide. They visited a market where people were buying various pieces of technology, and then saw an art exhibit. The interpreter pointed out a specific painting she seemed to like—a somewhat Impressionist rendering of a nature scene.

Kirk wondered about the planet's development. If they were all bound to one another's minds, how did art surprise or touch an individual who could have seen the conception of the work directly from the mind of the artist? After seeing another three paintings, all completely different, he decided to ask.

"Do you have a favorite artist, Captain?" she asked in reply.

He nodded. "A few."

"And do you enjoy their work only the first time you see it, or each time?"

Kirk smiled. "I see your point."

She continued walking and as they followed, she asked: "Are you an artist yourself?"

"Not by any stretch of the imagination," Kirk said with a smile.

If she didn't understand the idiom, she certainly got the gist of it and asked McCoy the same question. "Medical Officer, are you?"

The doctor shrugged. "I painted a little when I was younger."

She gasped in. "And did your paintings as conceived in thought translate to reality exactly as you intended?"

Kirk found himself picking up a few of the Isitri signs. The gestures for *yes* and *no* seemed to both precede and follow a question, making it clear an answer was being requested.

The doctor smiled. "Indeed they did not. If only they had."

The interpreter beamed the most charming smile. "As it is for you, it is for us. We are not very different."

The sign for *different* was one hand balled into a fist, and the other opened and palm up. Kirk liked it—how purely conceptual it was—and was beginning to see what Spock had admired about the manual language.

Next she took them to a recreational area, where mothers, fathers, and children were very obviously having a great deal of family fun. Watching them play was fascinating for Kirk—it was almost soundless play, but for the occasional chitter of laughter.

"They are learning," the interpreter said of the group.

"The children?" McCoy asked. "It's a school?"

"All of them are learning. About one another; skills from their parents; stories from one another. It's possible to focus on just the thoughts around you. We don't all communicate with everyone else, any more than you would speak to everyone you see simultaneously."

"But you can," Kirk said. "When one of these troublesome minds appears, the entire planet communicates."

"That is more limited communication," she replied, and her frown was deep. Isitri faces were amazingly expressive, and it was very clear to Kirk that neither sign language nor telepathy alone could fully convey their full range of emotion. The language was obviously a mixture of conceptual gestures, postures, expressions, and even some mime. "Since will and thought is one-way when a troublesome mind is in control . . . the communication is not the cacophony it would otherwise be to link *all* minds at once."

"So, when I speak to you, I'm not speaking to all Isitri?" Kirk asked after they walked a bit farther, and had begun a loop back toward the room where the council deliberated.

"You are not," she said. "Since I am currently telling only my husband of my experiences today. My memories, should I choose to allow them, will be read by others. But that is *my* choice." She emphasized *my* and the sign was a fist, centered on her chest and drawn down her trunk, stopping at her abdomen.

"Does anyone ever take your thoughts without asking?" As soon as the words were spoken, Kirk regretted the harsh tone of his pointed question. His habit was to be blunt, but the Isitri woman didn't seem fazed by it.

"The only time that is possible is should a troublesome mind touch my thoughts. Such was when Berlis visited with the council. As we explained, we can't be sure what memories he did or did not violate, because only once he was far enough away were we able to stir back into our own consciousness and wills." Her jaw quivered. "Exactly what happened while he was in control . . . parts are rather vague to us."

McCoy's face was quite expressive now, and mirrored Kirk's feelings. It was unimaginable: to essentially go into a mindless coma, become a zombie of sorts, while your thoughts—the essence of who you are—were violated by a telepathic dictator. Was that really what Berlis was? He'd seemed so innocent and childlike.

As they neared the council chamber again, McCoy asked a question that had been nagging at Kirk as well: "Pardon me, but Chista said Berlis might be unaware of the control he's exerting. How is that possible?"

The woman thought about it a long moment, then her jaw quivered, which Kirk now considered might be more of a shrug than a sigh. "My mind," she said finally, "is not troublesome, so I do not know for certain. But if he were intentionally controlling us, why would he have left, knowing his control would have ended once he was far enough away from Isitra Zero? He'd not been with us long enough for the link to last past his visit."

"So how did his control manifest itself?" Kirk asked.

"It is difficult to explain," she answered. "We knew he was directing our thoughts and our actions on some level, but could not really divide where our wishes ended and his began. His wishes simply became ours— our wills totally subverted."

Kirk knew he'd brought McCoy along for good reason: he asked another excellent question. "If you're not sure which thoughts were yours, how do you know any were his?"

She smiled tellingly, as if sharing an intimate secret.

"To this point, Medical Officer, the purpose of my existence was not to please Berlis."

McCoy chuckled.

"When he spoke to the council," she continued, "we all felt our purpose was to assist him and ensure his satisfaction. When he left, we went back to our respective wishes, and felt the hole in our lives that follows the release from a troublesome mind." Now her smile turned mostly sad. "I like Berlis," she told McCoy and then looked at Kirk. "But I don't know if I truly like him, or if he has subconsciously suggested that I should like him. *This* is the danger we cannot survive."

She nodded—she pushed away her head. It obviously meant she was excusing herself because she turned and walked back into the council chamber.

As soon as Kirk and McCoy returned to *Enterprise,* Spock reported that a large Isitri fleet was gathering. The captain took the command chair and McCoy slipped to his spot at Kirk's side. Spock remained at the captain's right, ready to consult.

"Number of craft?" Kirk asked. "Class of weaponry?"

"So far twenty-three vessels of varying ability; low-level phasers and class-four shields."

One-on-one, hardly formidable. Amassed? *Enterprise* could be badly damaged—perhaps even disabled in a full fight.

Kirk gave Spock the details of his discussion with

the Isitri Council, including their determination to kill Berlis at whatever cost.

Listening without interrupting, Spock merely nodded at various points. "We should be able to disable them before they reach Isitra Colony First," he finally said matter-of-factly.

Kirk looked sharply at his Vulcan first officer, who was looking intently at the small gathering fleet launching into orbit. "Are you suggesting we interfere, Mister Spock?"

"We already have," Spock said. "Had we not rescued Berlis from his impending death, this fleet would not be gathering now. Berlis and his colony will surely mount a defense. Hundreds, perhaps thousands, will die. If we disable the Isitri fleet now, those lives will not be forfeit."

There is a certain logic to the argument, Kirk thought, but not to the premise. It was totally unlike Spock to suggest this course.

"Spock, you can't be serious," McCoy said, his eyebrows arched in shock.

"Quite serious, Doctor," the Vulcan said impartially, clasping his hands behind him. "Since the Isitri fleet cannot attack Berlis directly, for fear they will come under his influence, they must attack from afar. Millions of Colony First citizens will be unnecessarily put in jeopardy."

Tension spread from Kirk's back to his shoulders

and neck. He examined Spock's features: calm, unemo-
tional, and detached as usual. Yet the captain couldn't
help but wonder if the Vulcan's link with Berlis hadn't
caused some lasting bias or remained loosely connected.

"No, Mister Spock," Kirk said. "We've meddled
enough."

"And should Berlis and his colony request Federation assistance?" Spock offered. "Are we not obli-
gated—"

"To what?" McCoy snapped. "Commit murder for
anyone who asks our help?"

"Killing in self-defense is not murder," Spock said.
"I have formed a hypothesis about Berlis and his power
and do not believe he is aware that he exerts force on
people's minds." Spock's black eyes burrowed into
Kirk's and then McCoy's. "You both felt the benevolence that Berlis radiates. It isn't deceptive."

"Spock," Kirk began, but his first officer interrupted.

"Sir, it is my opinion that while the Isitri may be
unable to train Berlis's mind, I could—perhaps—teach
him certain Vulcan telepathic disciplines that would
negate his inherent control of others." Coal-black eyes
pleaded for Kirk to listen to reason. "Do we not owe
him the chance to negate his inherent threat to his
people?"

It was a compelling argument. But was it Spock's,

or was Berlis still in there somehow? Kirk became acutely aware that the crew was beginning to follow the discussion with interest, and perhaps they wondered the same: Chekov's eyes were on his board, but he was surely listening. Sulu had turned slightly back, and at the engineering console, DeSalle was fully turned toward the command chair until Kirk's eyes flicked in his direction and the man twisted swiftly around.

"You want to risk a mind-meld with someone who takes over other people's minds?" McCoy challenged.

"Admittedly risky, but perhaps the only way to avert the death of the colony," Spock said.

"There's no official agreement to assist either side in this very *internal* Isitri conflict," Kirk said sharply. "I won't help the Isitri Council against Berlis, I won't help Berlis against the Isitri Council, and I won't risk losing any member of this crew to either."

Peripherally, Kirk noted McCoy's nod of approval, but the captain was studying his first officer's expression. The Vulcan looked from McCoy to Kirk.

"Is that a problem, Mister Spock?"

Without hesitation, Spock said, "Of course not, Captain."

Kirk took in a breath and nodded as Spock returned to his station. It was Kirk's intention to seek one more audience with the Isitri Council, perhaps even with the Odib ambassador; Uhura hailed the planet again.

At some point after McCoy headed to sickbay and as the Isitri fleet continued to make its way for Berlis's colony, Spock left the bridge. As soon as Chekov's console alerted him about a shuttle launch, Kirk glanced back to see the Vulcan was missing.

"Close the bay doors," Kirk ordered. "Dammit, Spock," he said under his breath.

Sulu and Chekov struggled with their respective consoles—each having controls that could have overridden any command.

"We're locked out, Captain," Chekov said.

"Aft view."

On the main viewer, *Shuttlecraft Copernicus* sped away at full impulse. "He's heading for the Isitri fleet," Sulu said.

Kirk felt his jaw tighten and his teeth clench. "Tractor beam!"

Scotty shook his head and pointed to DeSalle, instructing him to press a sequence of buttons. Scotty then checked a readout and shook his head a second time. "Impossible, sir. Disabled at the main conduit," he grumbled.

"We can't bypass," DeSalle said, frustrated.

"Sulu, maneuver us in front of him." Kirk gripped the arms of the command chair tightly. What was Spock thinking? He *must* still be in Berlis's thrall, Kirk thought. But was Berlis that powerful and inscrutable to so covertly control someone? Or did Spock merely have some residual subconscious imperative left in him that he was now responding to?

Jabbing at the navigation console repeatedly, Sulu eventually twisted back to Kirk, a cross of annoyance and frustration in his eyes and voice. "I can't get power, sir."

Unbelievable, Kirk thought, and was out of his seat and checking Sulu's console in one swift move. He pivoted toward engineering. "Scotty?"

The engineer smacked at the controls. "Aye, I see what he's done. I can't fix it from here."

Kirk hooked a thumb tightly over his shoulder. "Go." He looked over Sulu's and Chekov's respective shoulders. Weapons were available—both phasers and photon torpedoes. The Spock he knew wouldn't have been careless enough to forget to disable them, unless he was sure Kirk wouldn't open fire on the shuttle. Not much of a gamble for Spock to make, but at the same time, should Kirk make one? A phaser beam, well placed, could disable the *Copernicus,* but if off even a fraction, the small ship would be destroyed, and Spock with it.

"Anything?" Kirk asked Uhura. She shook her head but continued to hail the shuttle.

The decision to fire on Spock weighed on the captain, and he processed all of it quickly as he lowered himself back into the command chair. Spock read him well enough—Kirk wasn't going to risk killing his first officer. *At least not until he's back on board and I can wring his neck.*

"Come on, Scotty," Kirk said quietly through his teeth.

Sulu kept keying in the same command to his console, anticipating again and again the moment navigation would be restored.

"Mister Scott, sir," Uhura said finally, her voice trailing off as Kirk pounded at the comm button with his fist.

"Kirk, here."

"I can get you half impulse for now, sir."

"Not fast enough, Mister Scott."

"And the tractor beam. Best I can do."

"Work on the rest. Kirk, out." He thumbed off the comm and pointed to the blank starscape on the main viewer. "Do the best we can with the tools at hand, gentlemen."

Enterprise pushed ahead—slowly—but *Copernicus* was faster. All Kirk needed was to get into tractor range. He leaned forward, willing the impulse engines forward.

"Range?"

"Another four hundred thousand kilometers, sir," Sulu said.

"Get a lock as soon as you can, DeSalle."

"On it, sir. We're edging closer."

"Captain!" Chekov's thick Russian accent—and the

shock behind it—cut across the bridge. "There's an overload building in the shuttle's engine!"

A thick, heavy realization hit Kirk in the gut as he motioned Chekov toward Spock's sensors. "Confirm."

DeSalle took Chekov's navigation console as the ensign leapt over to the science station. Kirk twisted toward him as the blue light reflected off the young man's face.

"Confirmed, sir," he said, still reviewing the sensor data. "*Copernicus*'s engine is on manual overload and will explode in . . . two point two minutes."

Kirk's face flushed and his throat tightened; he looked at Sulu. "Range?"

Sulu just shook his head.

SIX

He's flying it into the mass of the Isitri fleet." Kirk wasn't asking a question, and was more talking to himself than he was to Chekov, but the ensign answered anyway.

"Yes, sir."

On the viewscreen, Spock's shuttle sped forward, maintaining a faster sublight speed than *Enterprise* could muster in her hampered state. Spock used that damage he had inflicted to his advantage.

Damn.

Kirk ordered Uhura to inform the Isitri of the situation—so they could at least attempt to move their fleet out of the way. He thought grimly that this was what his Starfleet instructors meant when they said the darkest command decisions were those for which one could never be trained. What was he to do now, knowing that the Isitri wouldn't be able to move the bulk of their fleet in time? Destroy Spock's shuttle before he destroyed it himself and took the Isitri fleet with him? The blast wouldn't decimate the Isitri ships, but they'd be highly damaged and open to attacks by the Odib, or perhaps Berlis's forces, if he had any.

"The Isitri say they're pinned in, Captain." Uhura held her earpiece in place as she received the message. "If they move closer to Colony First, they'll be within range of Berlis's control, and if they move away, they'll be closer to the *Copernicus* when . . ." Her sentence trailed off because it was both difficult to imagine, and impossible to ignore: The Isitri fleet were between a rock and a hard place—slavery or death.

Why was Spock doing this? That's what Kirk wanted to know. An answer would have to wait, and if Kirk couldn't pull off the plan that was starting to form in his mind, it would be moot.

"Mister Sulu, lock phasers on *Copernicus.*"

Sulu turned slowly back to Kirk, even as his fingers were tapping in the commands to his controls. "Power level, sir?"

It wasn't a question asked often. Full power was assumed unless otherwise specified.

As Kirk spoke, his throat tightened around the

words. "Full. I want a narrow beam, right into the shield generator."

It was tacitly understood that such a hit would knock out life support and likely decompress the shuttle, killing anyone aboard almost instantly.

Sulu and DeSalle exchanged a soul-searching glance, and Kirk was sure he heard the slightest gasp from Uhura.

The captain pounded the comm button on the arm of his chair. "Bridge to transporter room."

"Transporter room, Kyle here."

"Mister Kyle, lock on the *Copernicus*. You'll have a moment once her shields drop before Mister Spock is killed by the explosive decompression. I need you to grab him in that moment."

There was a long silence at the other end. Then, Kyle's answer came, *"Aye, sir."* Not "I'll try, sir," or "That's impossible, sir," but a simple acknowledgment that the task would be done.

"Stand by, Sulu," Kirk said, then turned to DeSalle. "Be ready on the tractor beam, too."

"Sir?"

The captain nodded to the growing dot on the main viewscreen that was *Copernicus*. "Destroying the shields will accelerate the overload of her engines. The ship will flare and momentum will carry the explosion into the Isitri fleet." Kirk shook DeSalle with a forbidding command: "Pull the shuttle away from the Isitri fleet before it explodes."

"That will mean pulling it toward us," DeSalle said cheerlessly.

Kirk nodded. "You'll have the same window Kyle does."

"Aye, sir." DeSalle turned back to the console and pounced on the controls, readying his calculations.

Chekov began a metered countdown to the shuttle's engine overload versus the range for both transporter and tractor beams. Thanks to both previous damage and Spock's sabotage, the trouble would be that while pulling Spock out and *Copernicus* away from the Isitri fleet, its shields would be incapable of protecting *Enterprise* from the explosion.

Droplets of sweat collected in the small of Kirk's back and he pulled himself slightly away from the back of the command chair. Times like these, he hated being the captain of the ship, not because he had to make difficult decisions, though those weighed on him, but because he couldn't be at the helm or in the transporter room, taking the actual steps to implement his own orders. Kirk knew his people were good at their jobs—among the best—and he didn't doubt their ability. But for him to sit and wait, not being the person carrying out the commands . . . usually that feeling was a mere tweak. Today it was a punch to the gut.

"Five seconds to range," Chekov called.

"Transporter room, stand by," Kirk said into the comm.

"Four . . ."

"Sulu, target sharp."

"Three . . ."

Kirk and DeSalle exchanged a tense look of mutual affirmation.

"Two . . ."

Apprehension clenched the bridge and Kirk's every muscle was ready to snap.

"Range!" Chekov said.

"Now!" Kirk ordered simultaneously.

As one beam of energy shot out from the *Enterprise*'s phaser banks, a tractor beam grasped at *Copernicus* and pulled it toward them. Kirk knew at the same moment Kyle was working to find Spock and whisk him away before he was ripped asunder. Three technological marvels, considered almost commonplace, on which so many lives now hinged.

Before Kirk could hear if Kyle had gotten Spock, *Copernicus* cracked open like a giant egg and pushed forth a massive bubble of plasma and white-hot energy. *Enterprise* was slammed back. She rolled away, creaking under the strain as support struts buckled and circuits sparked. The bridge lights dimmed and returned, but the ship continued to quake and rumble.

"Stabilize," Kirk ordered above the din.

"Trying, sir," Sulu called out as he struggled with the controls.

"Thrusters!"

"Captain!" Chekov's voice. "Shockwave now pushing Isitri fleet—toward the colony!"

On the main viewscreen, the torrent of energy dissipated and the Isitri fleet could be seen rolling awkwardly toward the gas giant and its several moons, one of which held Berlis's colony.

The Isitri had stayed out of whatever they knew Berlis's range to be, and now—thanks to the explosion that blew them off course—they might be within the radius of his control.

Kirk didn't have time to consider the ramifications and instead was pounding at the comm. "Transporter room!"

"Internal communications are down, sir," Uhura said as she waved the remnants of a smoke plume from her console. "Trying auxiliary circuits."

"Sulu," Kirk barked around an intake of the acrid air, "take the conn." Two steps later, he was in the turbolift, zooming toward the transporter room, where he faced Spock, who was still on the transporter platform.

"Spock . . ." Kirk rasped, but said nothing else. He wanted to say, "How could you?" and "What were you thinking?" but he didn't. Instead, he addressed one of the security officers standing by.

"Place Mister Spock under arrest," Kirk said flatly, watching Spock's unmoving expression.

Behind the captain, Lieutenant Prescott exchanged a look with Ensign Michaluk. The last thing either man expected when they woke up this morning was to put the ship's first officer under arrest.

Prescott stepped forward but Michaluk hesitated. "Ensign," Prescott whispered harshly. When the man didn't move, Prescott raised his voice just a touch. "Kevin!"

Michaluk finally snapped out of his trance and closed the distance between himself and Spock. "Do you want him in the brig, sir?"

Kirk considered it for a moment and pressed his lips together, nearly sighing. "No. Confined to quarters," he said finally.

Prescott and Michaluk both nodded. With one hand on his phaser, Prescott motioned to the door. Spock acquiesced without complaint and the three left Kirk silently studying the empty transporter platform.

Kyle observed the captain a moment and took in a breath to speak, but the bosun's whistle beat him to it.

"Transporter room," Kyle said after thumbing the comm button.

"Captain Kirk, report to the bridge, please," Sulu said.

The captain took two steps until he was near the console comm speaker. "Report, Sulu."

"The Isitri fleet has fallen into orbit of Colony First, sir," Sulu reported. *"The Isitri Council reports they've lost contact with their vessels and believe Berlis now controls them all."*

Kirk exchanged a grim look with Kyle. "I'll be right there," he said, thumbing the comm button twice. "Kirk to sickbay."

"Sickbay, McCoy here."

"Bones, Spock is confined to his cabin. I want him examined."

"I'm on my way."

Kirk nodded curtly, pounded the comm off, twisted on a heel, and stalked out.

Once the captain had returned to the bridge, Sulu explained more fully that the Isitri fleet had recovered from the shockwave and had not only failed to attack Colony First, but also took defensive positions around it. The captain's brows knit in contemplation. What would this mean? If the fleet now served Berlis, would they attack Isitra Zero? If they tried, should Kirk stop them? No matter what he may have unintentionally done by saving Berlis from his death sentence, surely Spock's actions had sealed Kirk's fate; he would have a hand in the affairs between Zero and First. And perhaps that was what Spock truly wanted, for Kirk still couldn't fathom that the Vulcan had acted in what amounted to an attempt at cold-blooded murder.

Kirk watched the Isitri fleet in their defensive orbits for a solid minute, and then turned to Uhura. "Lieutenant, get me the Isitri Council."

"Aye, sir."

There was a long delay, likely because the Isitri were still unfamiliar with Starfleet's more advanced communication protocols. When the picture finally wavered into view, Kirk saw only the female interpreter who'd worked with the council, but not Chista or any of the others.

"I'd like to speak with the council," Kirk informed her.

A slight smile tugged at her lips. *"You are, I assure you, Captain,"* the interpreter said.

Of course, the council did not need to be physically present, Kirk realized, which made his task more difficult. He was used to dealing with personalities, reading them and sizing them up, so he could project a version of himself that best suited the person with whom he talked. This was different. He couldn't see Chista's body language or facial expressions and couldn't gauge his honesty or feelings.

Straightening up in the command chair, Kirk wanted to be as delicate as possible. "Your fleet . . ." Kirk started to say, but wasn't sure where to take it from there.

"Yes, Captain. It is lost. It was half our operative ships. We have reserves, of course, but the odds would now be equal to what have become Berlis's forces." Her

sign language seemed more abbreviated than before. More curt. Perhaps more fatalistic.

Kirk had the urge to ask what he could do, even though he knew he could do nothing. And yet he felt responsible—especially for Spock's actions. "I'm sorry," was all he could muster.

"We appreciate that, Captain Kirk," the interpreter said and her expression was a mystery to him—neither sincere nor insincere, yet Kirk detected a slightly snide tone in the universal translator. It was probably his imagination, or a manifestation of his guilt. *"We must now deliberate as to how we will answer the Odib's demands under our obligations to the treaty."*

"We would be happy to mediate as a neutral third party, once formal first contact is made with the Odib," Kirk offered.

Her expression was dismissive. *"Thank you, Captain. We shall be in contact with you should we decide in favor of such a course."*

The communication ended, and the interpreter's visage was replaced with the starscape. In the distance loomed the gas giant, and Isitri Colony First's moon. Kirk watched the gas giant's satellite for a moment, as if he could see Berlis on Colony First, as if he could discern his true intent from afar. He wondered again if Spock was under alien control, or whether there was some logical reason for the Vulcan's actions that he just could not see.

It was time to find out.

When he arrived at Spock's quarters, McCoy was leaving. Prescott and Michaluk were each standing at either side of the door. Each had a sidearm, and Kirk wondered how long they'd hesitate before stunning Spock, if need be. How long would Kirk hesitate, for that matter? And worse, how had they gotten into a situation where Kirk needed to think about such things?

McCoy shook his head.

"Bones?"

"It's not him, Jim."

Kirk looked sharply at the closed door and back at McCoy. "Berlis."

"It's got to be."

"It's not Spock at all?" Kirk frowned.

"Well, it is, but a Berlis version of him. An influenced Spock, I suppose."

Considering the doctor's assessment, Kirk looked at the door again. "Can you explain that?"

McCoy sighed heavily. "Near as I can tell, Spock is in there—fighting for control if his neurotransmitter levels are any indication." His tone was dark, discouraged. "But the man I talked to isn't our Spock. He's totally concerned with the Isitri colony . . . to the exclusion of all else."

Attempting to destroy himself—and others—for the sake of someone as dangerous as Berlis . . . It was the antithesis of Spock.

"You have to help him," Kirk said finally, still looking past the guards at the door to Spock's cabin.

McCoy chewed his lip. When he didn't answer, Kirk looked at him.

"I don't know what I can do, Jim. Spock has blocked out Klingon mind-rippers. If he can't block Berlis's telepathy, I'm not sure how I can, short of killing him."

Kirk's jaw tightened and his hands balled into fists at his sides. "We can't lose Spock because I chose to answer a distress call."

"I'm sorry," McCoy began somberly, "but right now Spock is as lost to us as the Isitri fleet is to Chista."

SEVEN

On the contrary, Captain, I'm quite certain of my own sanity."

Kirk needed to see Spock for himself, and found it chilling that his first officer sounded so convincing. If he had not been told about Berlis's powerful telepathy, Kirk would have believed the Vulcan's sincerity. The full plight of the Isitri should they fully fall under Berlis's spell began to weigh on the captain's shoulders.

"Sabotage? Attempted murder? These are the logical actions of a commander in Starfleet?" Kirk couldn't help but press, to see if the rationality Spock usually wielded was in there, as McCoy had suggested.

"I attempted no murder," he said flatly, as if debating some small point in an insignificant matter. He sat at his desk, hands clasped on his lap, a picture of unruffled serenity. "I assumed your actions would result in the loss of the shuttle in a manner that would hamper the Isitri fleet."

"You could have died, and killed hundreds of others because of your actions."

Spock tilted his head down in acknowledgment. "I took a calculated risk with my own life, in the hopes of saving hundreds of others. That was my goal *and* the ultimate consequence."

"But *why*?" The *why* came out as a half growl.

"Berlis is an innocent," Spock said. "I have an obligation to protect innocent life. An entire fleet had set out to destroy one man who has committed no crime, other than posing a *possible* threat. Possible threats should never be treated as actual threats."

It was quintessential Spock in tone, and yet the logic had hemorrhaged. Kirk's lips curled around a question but he decided it was fruitless to ask to speak to the real Spock. There was no appeal to be made here, for such a request would have to be made to the man in control of Spock.

Pivoting quickly toward the door, Kirk left his first officer sitting, watching after him, the guards stepping back into view just as the doors closed behind him.

Spock was left to his thoughts. He was concerned for Kirk, but more so for Berlis. What would the captain do? Could he help the Isitri now? It would be a violation of the Prime Directive to do so, but Kirk had been known to make calculated risks regarding the edict. The odds that Kirk would interfere on the side of the Isitri, against Berlis, were close to twenty point seven to one, but those were hardly impossible odds.

The notion that bothered Spock for a brief moment was how disquieted both the doctor and the captain seemed by his completely justified behavior. While McCoy and Kirk were both prone to flights of fancy, generally at least one of them was more grounded in reality and morality. It was mystifying. He thought he might examine the reasons more fully, but decided that doing so would be futile and would take time away from formulating a just end to the Isitri question. Something must be done to save Colony First. Spock knew the Odib would not allow the treaty to go unenforced, and that being the case, Chista would not listen to reason.

Yes, something had to be done.

Once in the turbolift, the bosun's whistle prompted Kirk to hit the wall comm. "Kirk, here."

"I have Chista for you, sir," Uhura said.

"Patch it down here, Lieutenant."

"Aye, sir. Switching."

Kirk twisted the lift control handle and stopped its movement.

"Captain Kirk?" It was the universal translator's

voice, but Kirk imagined it was the Isitri Council's interpreter doing the speaking for Chista.

"This is Kirk."

"*I am Chista,*" the voice said. "*We spoke previously.*"

"I remember you." Kirk's lips curled into a small, tight smile. The greeting was quaint, as if Kirk could ever forget Chista under these circumstances. He wondered if it was something the Isitri felt was necessary for non-telepaths. Spock spoke of different minds feeling differently, and just as Kirk would recognize a voice, Chista probably identified people by their telepathic signature; without it, he had to announce himself.

"*We have discussed the situation with the Odib ambassador and quelled their fears for the time being,*" Chista said.

"You have?"

"*We are not comfortable with the fact, but we've misdirected the Odib, suggesting that Berlis has been neutralized.*"

"I see." Kirk found it interesting that in this culture, too, politicians wouldn't admit to telling a lie, even when it was obvious they were. "Suggesting" and "misdirected," indeed.

"*Had we not, they would be warranted to war against us, Captain. At least against the colony.*"

"The one you wanted to destroy?"

"*Not destroy,*" Chista said. "*We wished to make a surgical strike against Berlis.*"

"With your entire fleet?" Kirk didn't buy it.

"The fleet was gathered as a last resort. If we must lose our colony . . . well, we would prefer it to losing our entire planet."

Kirk nodded and sighed. Sadly, he understood Chista's difficult position and even felt somewhat responsible for his lie. But what would happen if the Odib found out they'd been misdirected? Would they destroy the colony and Isitra Zero as well? Kirk had pushed the Isitri down this path, and his first officer had helped to herd them along the way. . . .

It had never been more apparent how much Kirk needed his friend. More important, though, he didn't want to give Berlis the advantage of having Spock at his disposal and putting Kirk at a disadvantage.

The captain realized he was thinking of Berlis not merely as a problem for the Isitri but also as a personal adversary. He felt a pang of guilt, and wondered if such a feeling was the result of his part in all that had happened, or whether it was the residual effect of Berlis's telepathy—that feeling he'd had when Berlis was aboard.

Was Berlis's aura the one he had broadcast to Kirk, or was it simply the real him? If he was as innocent as he seemed, perhaps he could be reasoned with.

"I'm going to talk to Berlis," Kirk said, partly to himself and partly to Chista.

There was a pause before the interpreter replied,

as if great discussion had quickly ensued. *"We do not understand what this will accomplish, Captain."*

"Neither do I," Kirk admitted, rubbing his palms together somewhat anxiously. He hoped to convince Berlis to release Spock, though that wouldn't solve the Isitri's problem with their colony—or the Odib. But it would be a step in the right direction. "I'll let you know the outcome. Kirk, out." He thumbed off the comm and restored movement to the turbolift with a new command. "Transporter room."

After informing Scotty and giving him the conn, Kirk had Uhura request an audience with Berlis.

"He has transmitted coordinates for the Colony First council chamber, sir," she reported. A council was an interesting concept where Berlis was concerned. Did he alone sit at a large table? Then again, Chista could do that and still be in contact with his peers—or the entire planet.

When Kirk materialized on the colony, he was struck by the harsh contrast with Isitra Zero's council chamber. This building was less grand, and while not makeshift per se, one got the sense that it had been constructed more for purpose than style. The walls looked to be a quickly fabricated type of concrete and the floor was much the same, just painted a different color. The temperature was warm, but the hall was emotionally cold.

There was some artwork, but almost all of it looked

photographic—cold and uninspired. Drapes covered the few windows, and the Isitri sun shone in, casting a glare off the hard floor. Some small animal the size of a cat but shaped more like a giraffe—spindly with long legs and an extended neck—was lying in one of the light bars that streamed into the room. As Kirk approached it stood, startled, and ran off. As it skittered away he wondered if the Isitri could talk to animals telepathically, and if so, did the animals listen?

Then again, for hundreds of years on Earth there had been several higher primates that had been taught a sign language similar to that which the Isitri used. It wasn't inconceivable that Kirk had just seen a mini, telepathic giraffe.

When Kirk was summoned into the council's chamber, he was surprised to find the hall full of people. An official interpreter introduced himself first—unlike the Isitra Zero interpreter who never revealed her name. This man called himself Totrostav, and he explained the names and positions of each of the eleven people around the wooden table. There was someone in charge of water reclamation and someone who directed new housing fabrication, and so on. Several people had more than one responsibility. Interestingly, Berlis, who sat to one side rather than at the head of the table, went without introduction.

"Captain, it is good to see you once more," Berlis said through the interpreter. The cadence through the universal translator was certainly better articulated now than his own speech had been on the *Enterprise*. The universal translator had enough exposure to fluidly translate the language.

Berlis's smile was infectious, if not to Kirk, then surely to his own people—they all looked pleasantly toward him.

Kirk nodded at them, and then turned to Berlis. "I don't mince words," the captain said brusquely.

Brows knitted with confusion, Berlis looked from Kirk to the interpreter and back. "You will not . . . cut words into small bits?" Totrostav asked.

"I say what I mean," Kirk explained. "And I expect the same from my friends."

Berlis understood and seemed quite pleased with himself. He nodded cheerfully. "Oh, I agree, I agree. Speak clearly, and I will also."

"You've assaulted my first officer. You continue to do so. It has to stop," Kirk said, less harshly than he actually intended. He'd wanted it to sound like the accusation it was, but it came out more like an appeal.

"I do not understand," Berlis said.

One of the other colony council members lifted a hand to get Kirk's attention. "Berlis would not assault someone, Captain. You must be mistaken."

If Chista was correct, that was Berlis making an objection, and not the individual through whom he spoke. Had Spock's actions not been so uncharacteristic, however, Kirk would be wondering if Chista was telling the truth. Without being a telepath himself, how could Kirk know for certain what Berlis was or wasn't doing or of what he was capable?

"You're in control of Spock. He disobeyed orders to help you."

"He is a telepath," Berlis said. "We speak, but I do not control him."

Kirk squared his shoulders, hoping his body language would show his unwillingness to back down. "Your conversation is against his will."

"Of course not. I would never—" Berlis looked confused and hurt. "Captain, your friend only told me what the council on Isitra Zero decreed, and lamented with me about my plight. But I asked nothing of him."

Pulling in a tight breath, Kirk felt a rush of anger, and then quickly calmed down. He said evenly, "You're telling me he decided to ignore his oath so he could willingly support your insurrection—"

Jaw quivering, Berlis said, "There is no insurrection. We want nothing but to be left alone."

"Spock told you what we learned on Isitra Zero of his own accord?" Kirk asked.

Berlis gasped and the interpreter said, "Yes."

"Then you also know your people are in breach of their agreement with the Odib."

Bulbous eyes cast down, Berlis looked sadly at the table. "I had hoped to negotiate with the Odib myself.

To convince them I am no threat to them or to my people."

"Chista disagrees," Kirk said.

"I love Chista as I do the others from my home-world, Captain, but he is wrong about me." The sign from the interpreter for *but* was the same one that Chista's interpreter used for *different*. That made sense and he realized the gestural language was perhaps easily learned because it followed a conceptual logic.

Even without Spock, Kirk thought logic was key. Could he convince Berlis he was a threat—to Spock and to his own people? "Do you deny being a trouble-some mind?" he asked.

Berlis was forthright. "I do. I was never seen as such. Ever." He looked around the council table, indicating all seated. "People may like me, and may be inclined to help me when troubled, but I promise you I do not manipulate them."

"Why would Chista say otherwise?" Kirk pressed. "Why sentence you to death, and start a chain of events that would lead the Odib to annihilate your entire colony?"

Frowning, baring sharp little teeth that didn't appear when the Isitri smiled, Berlis looked an odd cross between menacing and sad. "I do not know. I met Chista when I visited Zero council. You would have to ask him. *I* would like to ask him."

"You've linked minds with him," Kirk asked, "but don't know him?"

"Someone reveals of themselves only as much as they wish. If Chista wanted to murder me, we could link minds and he could keep that from me as surely as you could keep from me your ill will by not speaking it." A series of gasps from the other council members indicated their agreement. "I am not your enemy, Captain," Berlis continued. "I am not Chista's or the Odib's. I only want to be allowed to live. Is that wrong?"

Kirk shook his head. "But if you're as dangerous as they say—"

"I wouldn't ask you to know Isitri law, but have I broken any moral absolutes that you hold?"

When Berlis spoke without the help of an interpreter, he had seemed innocent. Kirk thought that a more articulate Berlis would appear less so, but now he was more philosophical and . . . more logical. If Berlis was influencing Spock, was it possible that Spock was influencing Berlis—enough so that he really was less of a threat to the Odib and Isitra Zero? Or were Kirk's second thoughts influenced by this aura of trustworthiness Berlis radiated?

"You've broken no law or moral code, as far as I know."

"He hasn't, Captain," one of the others said. "And he has only ever been wise and helpful as our council leader."

Berlis stood. "What would you like me to do, Captain?" he asked. "I don't believe I've manipulated Spock. I'm merely charmed by such a creature as he. His telepathy stretches far, and his mind is refreshingly complex. He fascinates me. His culture fascinates me, and someday I'd enjoy meeting other Vulcans."

"What would I have you do?" Kirk leaned down, flattening his hands on the table. "Release your hold on him."

Berlis's breathy huff indicated, "No." He continued, "Were there a hold to release, I would." He sat back down and turned his gaze away, looking lonely, as if he were losing a friend.

Kirk was almost sure he felt that raw emotion radiating from him.

"I must ask you to go," the interpreter said for Berlis. "You are not the man I believed you to be."

Kirk's tight jaw opened to speak, but he was not sure what to say so he closed it again. Whatever power Berlis had was manifesting itself before him. He felt sorry for the alien, despite the anger he knew was welling within himself.

Kirk stoked that anger and let it grow until the sadness Berlis pushed on him was but a shadow. He curtly nodded and flipped open his communicator. "Kirk to *Enterprise*. One to beam up."

EIGHT

Spock lay tilted on sickbay's exam table. Desperate to free his first officer's mind from Berlis, Kirk had insisted McCoy use a chemical concoction normally employed by undercover security agents to protect their minds from telepathic invasion. It worked for many races, including Rigelians . . . but had never been tested on a Vulcan.

McCoy waved his scanner, looked at his tricorder and at the readouts. He did this at least three times before Kirk had to stifle the urge to bark at him. When the doctor grunted and shook his head at one of his scans, Kirk gave in.

"Bones?"

Spock opened his mouth to answer but McCoy stepped on whatever he might have said. "Damn it, Jim, I don't know! His neurotransmitter levels haven't changed, so I *just can't tell*! Let me work, and you'll know that much sooner!"

Lips pursing tightly, Kirk growled, "Hurry." He was unwilling to allow McCoy the last word.

Still, McCoy grumbled, "What I wouldn't do for a waiting room."

Kirk paced toward the desk, glanced into the open cabinet behind it and its mundane contents, and twisted back to Spock and McCoy.

"Okay," McCoy said, releasing the bed back into a vertical position. "I don't think it worked. If there were another Vulcan on board, maybe."

"Why another Vulcan?" Kirk asked.

"Because a chemical cure alone won't do it, but if Spock could muster his own defenses . . ." McCoy put the tricorder and scanner on his desk then turned back to Kirk. "If another Vulcan melds with him it might help."

With a slightly articulated brow, Spock disagreed and stepped to the deck. "No such defense is necessary, gentlemen—"

"The hell it isn't," McCoy said.

Suddenly Kirk rushed forward and harshly grasped Spock by the shoulders.

Surprise tainted Spock's normally cool visage as he stared into Kirk's angry eyes.

"Spock, you're in there and I'm *ordering* you to fight Berlis's control!" He shook the taller man, who despite his great strength did not pull away. "Do you hear me? *Do you hear me?*"

"Jim, you can't expect—"

Kirk silenced McCoy with a harsh glare and a shake of his head. He kept his grasp tight on Spock. The doctor's notion about Vulcan mind-melds reminded Kirk that Berlis and Spock were different races, and their telepathy, though similar, wasn't the same. If Kirk could use that difference—and force Spock to use it . . . "You're Spock, first officer of the *U.S.S. Enterprise*! You have a *duty* to assert yourself—to protect your ship against alien attack!"

Rather than answer the accusation, as anyone else might have, Spock was silent. His coal-black eyes peered into Kirk's severe glare. The captain shook him ever so slightly and ground each word through gritted teeth, "Fight, Spock. Fight for your own life!"

Neither man blinked. Arms pinned to his sides by the fervor of his captain's grip, Spock shuddered. It wasn't much, and might not have been recognized by McCoy, but Kirk saw it and felt the real Spock stirring from his slumber. "Yes!" Kirk spun Spock around so McCoy could see the Vulcan's face and stand witness. "Come on, Spock! Wrestle him! If nothing else—make him work for it! Make him struggle to hold on to you!"

Behind him, Kirk heard McCoy's scanner hum, but the doctor made no indication of a finding.

"Let go of him, Berlis!" Kirk demanded, his plan now twofold: strengthen Spock while weakening Berlis. There was a kindness to the Isitri man that couldn't be faked. Kirk would appeal to him—maybe even intimidate him into letting Spock go, or at least crack him enough to let Spock get through. "Let him choose, Berlis! Let him *decide* to be part of your hive-mind! You owe me that! You owe *him*!"

A flicker of recognition played in Spock's eyes— realization that something *was* wrong—that Berlis was exerting influence. That was when the battle began in earnest. Suddenly, in one fluid motion, Spock pulled out of Kirk's grip and locked the captain in a similar hold. *"I!"*

The pain inflicted by Spock's strong hands sizzled up Kirk's arms like lightning. He groaned but quickly recovered himself. "Yes, Spock! That's it. Take over. Shut him out!"

"I . . . *I* am—"

"Spock!" Kirk's voice was loud but sounded throaty and fatigued. Bruises were surely spreading from where Vulcan strength fixed his forearms to his sides. Pain radiated up his shoulders and into his neck. "You're first officer of the *U.S.S. Enterprise!*" Kirk charged. "You have a duty—"

"I—am—*Spock!*" the Vulcan yelled, and collapsed backward.

Darkness. Neither cold nor warm, a black womb enveloped him. His wish to stay within the protective cocoon was overridden by curiosity; whose voices did he hear?

"Bones?" It was the captain's name for Doctor McCoy, but the voice was distorted. Was someone else saying this? Spock analyzed the inflection, since the speaker's identity eluded him. However muffled and deformed the sound, he believed it *was* Captain Kirk.

"Chapel, get in here." McCoy? Logically it had to be him, but again the voice was oddly unfamiliar. The rest came and went in pitch, tone, and speed. It was an unnerving blur that with effort he could perhaps decipher, but the energy to do so eluded him.

"Respiration— . . . —olerance, Doctor."

"I can see th— . . . —cc's of nentizene!"

"What's happen—?"

"—rainwave patterns have alm— . . . —pletely shut down."

"—barely regis— . . . —nough to control— . . . —itals."

The words became less real, twisting into sounds that lacked cohesion and coherence. At one point, perception told him Vulcan was being spoken, but reason required he disregard that possibility. Clearly his mind had slipped into self-seclusion, and had seemingly taken his body with it.

With time—he couldn't be certain how much—Spock realized he had forced his consciousness to retreat away from Berlis beneath several layers of telepathic protection. Such a technique was prehistoric on Vulcan, used when ancient warriors pushed their minds into those of their enemies. He'd used a less severe adaptation of the procedure against Kor's mind-ripper on Organia, but here he'd needed the entire method to regain himself.

Now, with full realization of what had transpired, Spock was ready to pull back the unneeded layers. Not all the mental shields he'd raised were required, and determining which were necessary would take considerable review and testing. As he slowly lowered his defenses, more awareness seeped in from the outside world. He felt nerve endings come alive again and realized he was on his back, no doubt on Doctor McCoy's examination table. The temperature was an uncomfortably cool twenty-three degrees. There were three others in the room, seven in the corridor passing by, a turbolift opening seventeen meters away with two people (one male, one female human, judging from their respective heartbeats), and the captain was necessarily one of the people standing close by: Spock could hear the clicking of his tense jaw.

He waited approximately seven extra seconds before opening his eyes.

"—enough to control his vitals, sir . . ." Chapel's face looked to McCoy in shock. "Doctor!"

Spock sat upright, all eyes on him. As McCoy checked scanner readouts, the Vulcan met Kirk's quizzical brow with an arched one of his own.

"Spock?"

"Yes, sir," Spock replied.

"How—how are you?" Kirk asked.

"Quite well, now."

"But are you *you*?" McCoy demanded. "You fainted just a moment ago and—"

"Vulcans don't faint, Doctor," Spock said as he planted his feet firmly on the deck. "I was discerning the proper mental defenses needed to block Berlis from my mind, then erecting those barriers."

"It took thirty seconds?" Kirk asked, astonished.

Spock allowed mild surprise to taint his expression. "It did seem much longer, but I admit to needing to break off all base perceptions in order to . . . weed out that which did not belong."

A slight smirk playing at his lips, Kirk exchanged a knowing glance with Chapel. "That's Mister Spock," she said, and Kirk nodded once. It was.

"Now wait a minute," McCoy interjected. "Unless

we verify it's actually you, you saying you're fine now isn't worth a hill of beans."

"Indeed." Spock assented to McCoy's logic so quickly that the doctor showed signs of shock. He waited for the jab of punchline but none was forthcoming.

"So verify it." Kirk gestured McCoy toward Spock.

Lightly biting his lip and then playing with the ring on his little finger for a moment, McCoy finally grunted his inability to do just that. "Dismissed, Nurse," he told Chapel finally.

Bemused, she smiled knowingly, nodded, and left.

"I must apologize, Captain." Spock looked at Kirk, and yet slightly behind him.

He was embarrassed, Kirk realized, and to put his friend at ease, the captain also looked away. "Spock . . . It's not your fault," McCoy said, grudgingly. "He—"

Spock pursed his lips and shook his head grimly. "I allowed the initial contact; therefore, the fault *is* mine, Doctor."

"You *allowed*?" Kirk asked.

Lowering his head in assent, Spock pulled in a deep breath. "I did. I believed he had inadvertently contacted me telepathically. He was as curious about my alien mind as was I about his."

Kirk nodded. Sometimes his science officer gave in to his admirable curiosity in painfully ill-timed ways. "And then he refused to relinquish the link."

Thinking about that a short moment, Spock met Kirk's eyes. "Captain, I'm not sure he can."

"Explain."

"Even now it is taking great effort to maintain the mental protections that keep Berlis out," Spock said gravely. "And from my contact with him I believe he is not so much exerting force as he is giving in to his nature. To ask him not to contact minds in the way he does would be akin to asking you to hold your breath indefinitely. He might be able to do so for a short time, but eventually nature will out." The Vulcan looked from McCoy's sympathetic gaze to Kirk's stern one. "Should he attempt to press back into my mind, I may or may not be able to keep him out," Spock said. "I cannot be trusted."

"Spock," Kirk began.

"Captain, I won't be able to tell you should the barrier fall."

"I'll know," Kirk said.

"Jim," McCoy protested, "if *he* won't know, how could you? You're going to risk this ship on a hunch?"

It wouldn't be the first time, Kirk thought. "I'll know," he said adamantly. "We didn't know what to look for before. Now we do."

Smirking, McCoy nodded toward Kirk. "Again, he trusts his human intuition, Mister Spock. Considering how fragile the Vulcan mind is to Isitri telepathy, perhaps you should engage your human half. It seems the Vulcan half isn't as reliable."

"I assure you, Doctor, I will give your prescription all the weight and contemplation it is due."

Normally the interplay in such a situation would mildly annoy Kirk, but today it felt reassuring.

Less comforting was the thought that Spock could be lost again. "How far away do we have to take you," Kirk asked him, "for Berlis to be unable to reach you?"

"Unknown," Spock said after a moment's consideration. "Vulcan telepathy is generally contact driven, but as you know, there is a component that can traverse long distances."

Remembering Spock's reaction to the hundreds of Vulcans who died on the *Intrepid,* Kirk nodded.

"Well, I hope it takes proximity to make initial contact at least," McCoy said. "Otherwise there's an entire planet that Berlis could control from light-years away."

The thought loomed over them. Berlis had a fleet, and he had access to all Spock knew or, at least, was familiar with it. "If he traveled to Vulcan . . ." Kirk said.

"He would have a very formidable army," Spock replied. "We cannot allow that to happen."

Suddenly what had been a very local problem became galactic. "Would he?" Kirk asked.

"He might," Spock said. "Not out of malevolence, but self-preservation. That is the malignant element."

"What is?" McCoy asked.

"Through Berlis I was able to touch the minds of every Isitri on Colony First. They're conflicted. They love Berlis. He is a part of them. And yet, they no longer know where Berlis ends and they begin." His eyes looking away, farther than the opposite side of the room on which they focused, Spock's tone was low and almost somber. "I understand the horrific feeling. One doesn't so much stop being oneself as one is forced to ignore who one is and act on impulses not one's own. One's thoughts *seem* to be one's own . . . but they are not, and that only becomes clear when the troublesome mind is gone."

Kirk looked at his first officer. What was he to say? Spock had been imprisoned, in a way, against his will—on a very personal level.

The awkward silence lasted a little longer before Spock continued. "When I was linked to Berlis I believed I was acting on my own accord. I had no idea that my perceptions were so far removed from reality."

"What allowed you to realize differently?" McCoy asked.

"I didn't," Spock admitted. "I trusted the captain."

McCoy and Kirk shared a glance. That level of trust was what being in command was truly about—being able to lead someone not only down an unknown path, but also a seemingly wrong path, if the need called for doing so.

"My point, gentlemen," Spock continued, "is that Berlis is not so much coercing the Isitri colonists into being subservient as he is replacing their wills with an extension of his own. Only when he is gone will they realize they were not in control of themselves."

"It explains Chista's fear," Kirk said, rubbing his chin with the back of a thumb. "And it makes Berlis more dangerous. His people want him dead and he's reacting to it." He paced away, then back, considering the possibilities. "A cornered animal responds with panic. Berlis has become an actual threat because they tried to kill him when he was just a potential one."

"Berlis may be acting to save himself and his colonists," Spock said, "but *they* don't even know they have lost their free will. And should Berlis return to Isitra Zero, such will be the fate of billions."

"All because we intervened." McCoy shook his head dourly.

Kirk said as he marched toward the door, "And now we've got to stop him."

NINE

Sa-Gahnesaam, the Odib ambassador to Isitra Zero, had been kept waiting too long. In fact, being made to wait any longer from the instant he arrived was too long, and so the Isitri who asked him to wait was foolishly annoying him. What the Isitri didn't understand was how Sa was the calm, deliberative one among those in his government—at least as far as the Isitri were concerned. His superiors had decided to strike at the Isitri as soon as they were informed of the troublesome mind's existence. Sa-Gahnesaam convinced them to wait, since the problem was contained on the Isitri colony and their main planet was protected. While this contingency was not accounted for in the treaty, it made sense to not waste the resources, or the lives, by obliterating the Isitri.

Some in the forum believed Sa was naïve. He'd not lived through any of the Isitri wars, and did not know firsthand the fear that his forebears felt. But he had learned long ago—it was taught in school—of the horror of an enemy under the direction of a single mind. The Isitri, under a troublesome mind, were relentless, making their most active and intense technological bursts in such times—either because of war itself, or sheer will.

Conversely, the last Odib dark age was when they had to defend themselves at the expense of the planet's entire economy and a third of its population. The Odib had only now, after centuries, completely recovered. What a price they had paid for having brought the Isitri space flight. No, they would not allow themselves to be attacked again.

When the Isitri Council finally deigned to see him, Sa-Gahnesaam had worked himself up into quite a froth—he was annoyed for being kept waiting, and angry at the situation itself. He was also angry at his own hesitation. Sitting there, contemplating the choices he'd made, he decided he should not have lobbied to delay the launch of his people's fleet. Das-Dosiame had warned him against lobbying for postponement, and was, as usual, correct.

Sa marched into the council room and the interpreter greeted him on behalf of the group. He sneered at the slight little man and looked directly at the one whom he knew to be the leader. "Madam, give me news."

The interpreter began to gesture and his wrist device ground out choppy Odibian. "Chista informs that the troublesome mind threat has been neutralized."

"And what of his alien allies?"

"There are no allies. The Federation people have also communicated with Chista and our sister council. Their interference was a mistake they regret. They wish to open trade negotiations with us, and with you as well."

"I see." Sa-Gahnesaam narrowed his gaze, leveling it at the council chairwoman. "Are you certain?"

"Of course."

Having visited Isitra Zero for many years, and being intimately familiar with the people—especially this particular council—Sa was almost sure he was being lied to. He stroked his beard and studied her body language. She was nervous. In fact, the entire group of them looked like a nest of Istacha hatchlings, newborn and shaking. Even the interpreter was uneasy.

"Very well," the ambassador said cautiously. He could get nothing more out of them. But the Isitri, by nature of their telepathy, were very bad at keeping secrets. As he turned to leave, he knew he'd discover the truth soon enough.

A few hours passed before he could meet his contact. The notion of having spies on Isitra Zero was a dangerous one. As difficult as it was to keep state secrets, it was equally as thorny for a spy to stay concealed. But some Isitri—perhaps many—were as concerned as the Odib were about a troublesome mind coercing the populace. Many sympathetic minds probably looked the other way if they had an inkling of espionage, especially when the spy was as old as Sketel.

Sketel had lived through a war with the Odib, and so personally knew the horrors of Isitri slavery. In his case, he went to bed a little boy and when the troublesome mind was finally dead, he awoke to find his parents long passed, years of his life missing, and married to a woman he didn't really know or love. She was pregnant with their second child. He knew them intimately—and yet did not.

Because of this, he was invested in helping the Odib, not just for moral reasons, but for a very emotional one.

When Sa-Gahnesaam met him at his home, the look on Sketel's face told him there was indeed more than what the council would admit.

The Odib ambassador had years ago learned the Isitri sign language and he greeted Sketel traditionally: open palms clasped to heart, proving he held no weapon and had only his hands to protect his vital organ.

"Good see you," Sketel said.

"Same," Sa replied as his friend guided him out of the chill night air and into his flat.

Sketel doubled his frail form onto a padded bench and gestured to the seat opposite him. "Sit please, rest."

"Thank you." The ambassador pulled off his long coat and folded it neatly across the back of his chair before reclining.

Sketel kept his heat up quite high, and already Sa could feel himself beginning to perspire. With the sleeve of one hand he dabbed at the clammy skin on his head and with the other he unfastened the collar of his tunic and pulled his long beard away from his neck, exposing his chest to the air.

Sa took in his surroundings and told Sketel he had a lovely home. Like most of his people, the man seemed to like bright, primary colors. The floors were painted yellow, the walls orange-red, and much of the furniture was upholstered in a quilted fabric the color of the sea grass Sa's mother fed him as a boy. In these difficult times, it made him homesick.

Otherwise, Sketel's home was much like an Odib home—except for the one thing that always made an Isitri residence look a little odd. Sa's own house was filled with books—some old and printed, others newer and digital, but books were an important part of Odib life. Although he'd long understood the ways of the Isitri, the lack of books in their homes and offices always seemed strange.

Sketel offered him a drink, but Sa huffed his refusal. "You give help me again please," he said. He was blunt with his friend, as was the shared Odib and Isitri custom. That was one of the things he'd learned to admire about the fragile race: their need to cut to the heart of most matters.

Eyes bulging more than usual, Sketel's worried expression spoke to the difficult times before them, and the hard choices to be made. He gasped. "Know know."

"Tell me," Sa suggested, already certain Sketel would do so.

As if releasing a high-pressure valve, the old Isitri man began gesturing furiously fast. He had always been a signer, as he had a cousin who lacked telepathic ability and as children—that is, when he remembered being a child—they had played together. In fact, he was one of the Isitri who'd helped the Odib ambassador learn the manual language.

But the torrent of concepts flooding toward Sa-Gahnesaam became a mishmash. Once he'd lost the context the movements lost all meaning because there were too many signs that meant more than one thing depending on circumstance. The movement one made for *correct* was the same for *proper* and the same for *right* and the same for *moral* and the list could go on to cover several related ideas that were just slightly different. Within a sentence about which he knew the topic, Sa understood plainly which meaning was correct. In a contextual vacuum he couldn't know exactly what Sketel was saying. And when he struggled with one sign, the next three went unnoticed until random words just blended into panicked arm movements.

"Slow," he told the old Isitri man. "Please slow."

Starting again, Sketel moved at a speed that seemed more in tune with his age. He told him what he knew: that Berlis was still alive, that the aliens from outside the Home System had twice stopped the troublesome mind from being terminated, and that Berlis now had control of several Isitri fleet vessels.

Sa-Gahnesaam looked down for a long moment, and then finally met his friend's gaze. "You know what I must do."

Sketel gasped that he did. The man was neither naïve nor stupid and he long ago told Sa he'd come to terms with what would probably be seen as treason by many people.

"I would like you to come with us when the embassy staff leaves the planet," Sa told him. "I cannot guarantee your safety otherwise."

Eyes cast downward, Sketel laid his head sideways on his own shoulder and the slightest whine came from his nostrils.

"I know, my friend," Sa said. "I know."

But Sketel was looking away and the ambassador had to tap the Isitri man's leg to call his attention back.

"Is there no other way?" he asked.

Sa wished there was. "I will delay things as long as I can. You, and the others in the underground, must join us until . . ." He frowned. "Until the situation is concluded."

Signing slowly, making small, tired gestures, Sketel said, "Yes, of course. We will gather and meet you at the appointed hour."

There was an indescribable sadness in the old man's expressions, or maybe Sa-Gahnesaam was projecting his own mixed feelings onto his friend. It was so easy to be frustrated with bureaucracy and councils and politicians on both worlds—and so difficult to reconcile the problems they created with the people who just wanted to live their lives. It was difficult to not feel regret when dealing with people who'd become friends.

Sa thanked his friend for the information—and for his many years of counsel—and told him he hoped they would be able to save as many lives as possible. They both stood up, and the Odib ambassador put his chin on the old Isitri's head. It was a gesture of endear-

ment among Sketel's kind, a sign of affection a father
might show to his son, and despite the age difference it
seemed very right to Sa.

Back on the street again, his coat around his shoulders, Sa pulled a communications device from his
pocket. He looked at the small screen. SECURE FRE-
QUENCY it blinked.

Did he want to place this order? With his own
people he'd lobbied against such drastic matters, even
as he used them to threaten the Isitri.

What other choice was there? The treaty had been
broken and the peace was in jeopardy.

He opened the channel. "Prepare to evacuate the
embassy," he said with more sadness than he intended
for his aide to hear. "We must pull our people, and our
friends, home . . . and let our fleet do as they must."

Has the Enterprise *left the area?* Berlis asked the community at large, unsure of who might be monitoring
the skies.

A captain in one of the freighters replied: *They are
in visual range.*

Heartrendingly painful, but not unexpected. As
soon as Spock was no longer in his sphere, he felt it
was less likely that he was gone from the star system
than that Captain Kirk had convinced Spock to lock
himself away. Berlis had felt his Vulcan friend's internal

doubt—and then nothing. If only Berlis had been able to reassure Spock . . .

He didn't blame Kirk, really. Berlis understood the fear of the unknown. It was the same fear he had felt from the colonists regarding the difficult times ahead.

The problem that Spock's absence presented was one of information. He'd been a conduit to knowing what was occurring outside of Colony First. Without that channel, Berlis needed to improve the scope of his people's communications ability. He'd asked them to focus on improving their capability, and to his delight, their devotion produced a flurry of activity. It was one of the strengths of the Isitri, when they collectively had the will to work on a common goal: the ability to share knowledge and ideas almost instantly.

Pride washed over him, softening the dejection over losing Spock, but not eliminating it. He truly missed the Vulcan's calm, ordered mind. He'd taught Berlis much—not just about the Federation and the *Enterprise,* but also a more reasoned, logical philosophy. He didn't wholly embrace Vulcan philosophy, but admired Spock's devotion to it, and saw in it useful concepts he could draw on for his own life. Yes, his link with Spock had surely been an advantage, only somewhat diminished by its absence.

When Bithnush, the chief communications specialist this season, told Berlis that the upgrades were complete, both were overwhelmed with contentment—for a brief moment. As system improvements came online, that warm feeling crumbled away. A message from the Odib ambassador to his homeworld spoke of war. Berlis asked that the message be confirmed—spoken language could often be misinterpreted since no Isitri spoke out loud and many could not hear.

After checking three times, there was no doubt as to the communication's meaning or significance. A debate began instantly as to Colony First's next action. It would take a few days for an Odib fleet to arrive—if they were not already gathered and ready to deploy. Logic suggested they would be; therefore, time was of the essence. With half the Isitri fleet unwilling to protect the colony, how could Berlis hope to protect his people? And what of Isitra Zero? Would the Odib be satisfied with conquering the colony or would they move to the homeworld and attempt to end all threats they mistakenly perceived? Berlis understood that great wrongs had been done to the Odib in the past, and he was sympathetic to their trepidation. But he could not let them destroy his colony nor could he allow them to have a base from which to launch attacks on Isitra Zero.

His only option was to appeal to Chista's reason. They must join together against this common threat. Surely Chista and the council would agree.

It was decided: Berlis would go to the homeworld,

and convince the council that he was no threat—that the Odib were the current danger, and Colony First and Home Zero must work together.

Berlis was sure his people would listen to reason. When he appealed to them personally in the past, they'd always been amenable.

TEN

"Movement, Captain." Spock hovered over his scanners, where he should be, where it felt right to have him, Kirk thought. "Berlis is moving several ships toward Isitra Zero."

"On screen."

The forward viewer came to life, wavering as it magnified in on the gas giant moon that held Colony First. Several Isitri fighters rolled out of orbit and sped away.

Spock didn't believe Berlis's people had the ability to overhear the Odib communication *Enterprise* had intercepted. At least it wasn't his impression when he was linked with Berlis. But, there was a possibility that their capability would quickly progress, in a leap of technological improvements.

As Kirk watched the Isitri vessels shrink on the screen, he knew Berlis was aboard one of them—he could feel it. And if Berlis was taking a large fleet with him . . . when he got to Isitra Zero he'd have a whole fleet, and in fact an entire planet, at his command.

Kirk couldn't allow him to succeed. He'd helped put these events into play and he couldn't let his missteps lead to the destruction of two cultures. "Sulu, pursue the Isitri colonial fleet."

"Aye, sir."

Enterprise pushed herself quickly toward the fleeing vessels and on the main viewer they grew larger as the distance closed.

Spock kept himself locked on his sensors. "Several of the ships have turned to intercept us."

"Full shields." Perhaps because of his familiarity with Kirk through Spock, Berlis had obviously anticipated his pursuit. "Contact Chista," Kirk ordered Uhura. "Let him know Berlis is on his way." From the periphery, the captain saw Spock had turned toward him and so he swiveled in the direction of his first officer. "You disagree Berlis is aboard one of them?"

Spock shook his head. "Eminently logical. The fleet must stay with him, and he with it, if he is to keep control of them."

That begged a question Kirk hadn't considered before. "Then why didn't the colonists realize they had been under Berlis's control when he was away on Isitra Zero?"

"The longer a troublesome mind has influence, the more extended an amount of time an individual must be out of his sphere before his own will returns," Spock stated matter-of-factly.

Kirk rose and brought himself to the rail between them. "So it would have been more difficult for you to block him, the longer he'd been controlling you? Does he know that? Does he act on that fact, to increase his ability to direct people?"

Spock closed the distance between them. Kirk was suddenly reminded that his Vulcan friend *did* have emotions, though he rarely allowed them to surface. There was still some embarrassment around the topic of Berlis's control, of course. "It may be something he's subconsciously aware of," Spock said quietly.

As much advantage as Berlis might have knowing Spock, and Kirk through him, Kirk could now use Spock's knowledge of Berlis to his benefit as well. "You're saying he's a dictator who doesn't know he's dictating?"

"Essentially. I don't believe he acts deliberately to keep people in his sway, but intuitively he knows which actions will work in his favor." Spock nodded at the main viewer to indicate Berlis beyond it. "He knows that personal interaction works to his advantage, the same way a child discerns his parent will frequently acquiesce to tears. Does a toddler *seek* to manipulate or merely instinctively know how?"

"This isn't a child, Mister Spock."

Skeptical, Spock tilted his head. "You felt the innocence he radiates. I touched it with my mind; it is not a deception. In a very literal sense he is emotionally a child. How would you have matured if from a young age your mere presence influenced your elders *and* your peers into accepting your suggestions and eventually your whims?"

"He's a *spoiled* child," Kirk scoffed.

Spock shook his head and casually clasped his hands behind his back. "A benevolent despot, who only knows his own benevolence, and none of his despotism."

"Almost within weapons range, Captain." Chekov's voice wasn't tense, but heavy with anticipation.

Kirk turned fully toward the main screen and Spock returned to his station.

"I want them disab—"

"Their engines—" Spock called urgently.

Before them, the screen flared white. The three Isitri fighters didn't fire on *Enterprise,* but rather erupted in massive explosions. Force and momentum crashed debris and hot plasma energy into them, twisting the ship back and to its side. She fell off course.

Sparks sizzled around Kirk as the lights dimmed and relit. His lungs filled with the acrid smoke that billowed from a substation to the left. Sounds filled his ears beyond the straining of the engines against the shockwave. Bulkheads creaked and voices called out:

"—decks five, six, and eight! Damage teams respond!"

"—negative gravity, section thirty-seven beta!"

"Starboard support strut, four-three-two gamma!"

"—porter room, please respond!"

"Casualty report! Sickbay, come in!"

"All three vessels self-destructed in our path, Captain," Spock said.

This was an escalation Kirk hadn't predicted—but should have. If Spock, while under Berlis's thrall, was willing to sacrifice himself, why wouldn't the captains of those ships? And their crews? How many died? Hundreds. And they didn't even know it wasn't their choice. Was that a blessing, or a curse?

"Status of his fleet?"

"Sensors obscured by radiation," Spock reported.

"Uhura—" Kirk barked through the sounds of the extraction fans as the smoke cleared.

"Clearing channels for Mister Scott, sir."

Static crackled from the speaker on Kirk's chair arm. *"Shields compromised,"* came the harried Scottish accent. *"Auxiliary power is holding, sir, but we've got seven plasma coolant leaks and until we seal 'em there'll be no main engine output."*

"Understood." Kirk thumbed the comm off. There was no use pressing Scotty for schedule adjustments. Games with time management weren't useful in such dire situations. The captain spun toward communications where Uhura was under the lip of her console, bypassing circuits manually. "Lieutenant?"

"Working on it, sir." She knew they had to contact Chista before it was too late.

Kirk twisted toward Spock and launched himself against the rail. "Sensors?"

The Vulcan moved switches and hit buttons on his console, but above him the screen remained cut with blank static. "Negative. Radiation from the explosions."

"Distance to Isitra Zero?"

"At last measurement, approximately five point one six A.U."

The bridge was hot and Kirk was sweating. He wiped beads of perspiration from his brow and looked at the blank main viewer, mentally eyeing ships he couldn't see. "Under eight minutes at half impulse."

With calculation unnecessary, Spock said, "Or three minutes at warp factor one."

The captain nodded and pivoted toward the turbolift. "I'm taking a shuttle."

Uhura uncurled herself from under her console to watch the captain; the entire bridge crew turned toward him as well.

"Alone?" Spock stepped toward the turbolift.

"No, but I need you here," Kirk told him, and kept his own counsel about his feeling that the farther Spock was from Berlis, the better. "Sulu, you're with me. Spock, you have the conn."

Quietly, Sa-Gahnesaam had gathered his staff on the embassy roof. Sketel and a handful of other Isitri had joined them. Some from the underground refused to leave Isitra Zero. Many of them would not prepare for the war in any way—they went about their daily lives the same as usual. That was probably for the best, if Sa was to keep his leaving a secret.

Others were less discreet and took their families to rural areas to wait out the storm that was to come. While he'd have preferred they simply join his people on Odib, he understood their reasons against it. Living on an alien planet—as Sa had chosen to do—was a very unique circumstance and required a specific personality, especially if the communication barrier was such that one could interact only with relatively few people.

Still, he would have rather they come with him than overtly be seen moving away from large cities, especially the capital. While Sa trusted them all not to reveal that the Odib fleet was on its way, he knew loyalty to their bond might not matter on a planet where information traveled telepathically.

"I'm sorry, my friend," Sa signed to Sketel as he

ushered him and the other Isitri toward the small Odib craft.

Sketel shuffled close to Sa and faced him, the oddest expression on his features. The ambassador wasn't sure how to describe it. Melancholy? Detachment?

"Are you all right?" Sa asked.

"No," Sketel said. "And *I* am sorry."

Sa-Gahnesaam saw the Isitri's eyes narrow and his flat little nostrils flare with a grunt. Then he noticed the warm wetness spread across his own belly. Confused, he looked down to find Sketel's arm extended, holding the hilt of a knife that was buried between his ribs.

Eyes wide, Sa's jaw dropped. Peripherally he saw others attacked in kind—for each and every Odib there was one Isitri with a blade.

"No," Sa said as his life began to drain. Hot slices carved into him, he huffed out "No" in Isitri before falling to the floor like the rest of the slaughtered Odib embassy staff.

It didn't really hurt, Sa realized. He just felt the heat and moisture of his own blood and the shock of the moment. As his vision dimmed, Sketel's sad expression was the last face he saw. He expected to feel anger or hatred, but instead he simply grieved for his loved ones—including Sketel.

"I sorry," he saw the old Isitri man sign. "Rest well."

Darkness followed. And then oblivion.

• • •

The shuttle launched through the debris field left by the Isitri ships. Bits of wreckage snapped against the shields or sizzled in the deflector beams as they drove toward Isitra Zero.

"Sensors clear," Sulu said as they warped away from the radiation radius that cloaked the *Enterprise.* "Isitri fleet is . . ." Surprised, the lieutenant looked up from his console. "Not within range."

Kirk grabbed the sensor dome and looked for himself. "Where could they be?" He was asking himself, not Sulu or either of the two security guards behind them.

Shrugging his shoulders, Sulu offered his best guess: "On the planet?"

It was possible. In fact, if the Isitri fighters had been damaged by *Copernicus*'s explosion, and again by the shockwave of their own sacrificed ships, they'd need repair. Obscured by atmosphere and powered down, *Newton* wouldn't be able to find them with her sensors.

What awaited Kirk on Isitra Zero would remain a mystery until he arrived.

Sulu piloted ably, but Kirk fidgeted in the copilot's seat since one wasn't necessary on such a short trip.

The radio silence didn't help matters. Kirk couldn't raise the *Enterprise,* as her comm systems were still out, and Chista was not returning hails.

But there were standard navigational beacons that

acted normally as they approached the planet, which reassured them somewhat. It struck Kirk that Berlis might have intercepted Kirk's initial warning to Chista, and that in an attempt to avoid conflict with his own people, Berlis might also have directed his half of the Isitri fleet toward the Odib system. Tactically it wasn't an unsound idea. Berlis would have the advantage of surprise.

As they skimmed over the Isitri capital, Kirk couldn't help but notice how much like other cities—Earth cities—it looked: some tall buildings, some short; parks and streets; houses and apartment buildings.

They landed near the council building. Kirk, Sulu, and one of the security guards were greeted by the same interpreter who'd met him and McCoy previously. She wasn't surprised to see them.

"The council will see you immediately," she said, and led them to the chamber without another word or gesture.

Kirk and Sulu exchanged an uncomfortable glance as the door was opened for them and the interpreter led them in.

Chista welcomed them eagerly, apologetically. "Captain, I'm so sorry we didn't respond to your communication. You can imagine our surprise when Berlis returned, and he and the council were having words, as you can imagine."

Stepping to the side, Chista revealed Berlis's slight

form seated at the council table. "I heartily regret any loss of life from our encounter, Captain, but we did need to delay you so that Chista and I could meet and resolve our differences."

"And you've done that?" Kirk asked cautiously.

"We have," Chista assured him.

Kirk steeled his gaze, trying to pin Berlis with a glare. "And the three vessels you ordered to sacrifice themselves to delay me?"

"I made no such order, Captain," Berlis said sadly. "I asked the captains of those ships to impede you, but didn't think they would go to such lengths. I only wish they had not."

Kirk's shoulders were tight with tension; he didn't believe it. It was the first time Berlis had clearly lied, and judging by the slight flush of his pale Isitri skin, even he didn't believe what he was claiming.

Chista, however, trusted Berlis fully. "I understand why they did, Captain," he said. "They understood what I hadn't until Berlis explained. The Odib are the real threat."

On his first visit to the Isitri Council Kirk had noticed how the interpreter's tone had changed according to each person for whom she was signing. It may have been his imagination, but Kirk thought these differences between speakers were now gone.

The only indication that Chista was the one speaking was his animated body language and facial expressions. "While I had not upon first meeting, I cannot express how thankful I am that you intervened and kept Berlis from our foolish death sentence."

Chista smiled, Berlis smiled, the interpreter smiled, and the gathered council smiled. Likely, the entire planet smiled.

Except for James Kirk. His voice low, he only said, "You're welcome," and turned and left.

ELEVEN

In the time it took for *Shuttlecraft Newton* to return to the *Enterprise,* the radiation had cleared and enough repairs were completed to give Kirk's ship back her sight.

After checking on casualties in sickbay, he and McCoy made their way to the bridge.

Normally a discussion of options would happen in the briefing room, but for Kirk it would feel more like they were sitting around doing nothing, and he wanted to be doing *something.* On the bridge, where he could watch the tactical displays, he felt ready to pounce into action.

As they debated, however, all the captain really did was helplessly watch as the remainder of the Isitri fleet slowly achieved orbit. On another screen, telemetry probe data indicated the Odib fleet gathering itself as well. Soon they would make way . . . and then there would be war.

"What if we just beam him up?" Chekov asked. "Go to warp before they can react and he'll be too far to influence them."

It wasn't a bad idea—it just wasn't a workable one. Kirk had thought of it on the return shuttle trip. He'd ordered Spock to put priority on any transporter-related system knocked out by Berlis's suicide ships.

But after investigation Spock determined it wasn't feasible. Kirk looked to him to explain that to the ensign.

"Scans indicate that because of the war readiness demanded by Berlis, the Isitri government has been moved underground. The complex is beyond transporter range."

"And the longer he's in control," Kirk added, "the longer it will take for the Isitri to reassert their own wills." The captain shook his head soberly. "We beam him away and go to warp—and an entire fleet will pursue us."

Sulu was turned from the helm and seemed to meet both Spock's and the captain's eyes as he asked, "Could we stop the Odib fleet, somehow? Remove the reason Berlis is going to deploy *his* ships?"

"Now wait a minute," McCoy interrupted. "What

are we talking about here?" He stepped closer to Kirk. Arms crossed, the doctor took on an indignant pose. "Maybe we stop both sides from killing each other, but then what? Become Organian-like referees, imposing our own treaty?"

Pulling in a long breath, Kirk rose, looked at McCoy a moment, then stepped around the helm and glared at the main viewscreen. Engines were minutes away from coming back online. *Enterprise* could go anywhere then, and if she left, there wasn't a regulation that could be tossed in Kirk's face for leaving the situation as it was.

Except his conscience.

"We started this landslide," Kirk said, still watching the planet and the assembling Isitri fleet. "Now it's about to become an avalanche."

"Jim, you can't fight their war," McCoy protested.

"I wasn't planning to." Kirk pivoted toward his first officer. "Spock."

The Vulcan rose from his seat as Kirk approached. "Captain?"

"Your mind-link with Berlis. Was it two way?" Kirk leaned against the lip of Spock's station. "He learned about the *Enterprise,* the Federation. Did you learn about him? About Isitri history?"

"I did," Spock said. "Much of the information would have been subconsciously transferred, but I believe I can access it. Have you something specific in mind?"

The captain shook his head tiredly. "I do. Other

troublesome minds. How were they handled? Surely all their reigns didn't end when they died of old age."

Spock considered the question for a moment, as if searching some mental database. "Some did have accidents, or were murdered in power struggles," he offered. "And two were killed by the Odib."

There wasn't much Kirk could do with that information. He paced back toward his command chair, all eyes on him. "He *must* have a weakness."

"Certainly," Chekov said. "Is he not basically humanoid? He could be poisoned, phasered, stabbed—"

Kirk sneered. "*Without* killing him, Ensign."

With a shrug, Chekov turned quietly back to his console, pulling his hands from his lap and placing them on the controls.

"Mister Chekov is not incorrect," Spock said. "In the past, some did die of poisoning."

An idea stuck Kirk and he spun toward Spock. "Wait a minute."

"Jim, you can't be thinking—"

"Hold on, Bones." Kirk was on to an idea and needed to follow it through, uninterrupted. "Spock, how could anyone attack someone like Berlis? Why wouldn't he know as soon as someone planned such an execution?"

Silently, Spock considered the question.

"Well, Spock?" McCoy prodded after several long moments.

"Forgive me, Doctor, this is not exactly as easy as accessing the information on the library computer." Spock closed his eyes, then opened them again. "Captain, there is a danger to searching for such specific information."

Kirk and McCoy exchanged a brief glance. "What kind of danger?"

"To access these . . . memories, I will have to break down certain barriers . . ."

"You'll have to link with Berlis again?" McCoy asked.

"No. But there is a chance, if he is attempting to link with me, that he might succeed. The effort it takes to keep him out will be otherwise diverted."

McCoy stepped toward the captain and demanded his full attention. "Jim, if we lose him to Berlis how will we know? He could give us wrong information. Or tell us only what Berlis wants us to know."

The logic gnawed at Kirk. What strange set of circumstances had led them to this point: where McCoy was the voice of reason. Despite the fact he was right, Kirk hammered the doctor with a sharp glare.

"Right," McCoy said sarcastically. "You'll just know."

"I agree with Doctor McCoy," Spock said. "Should we attempt this, we should retire to sickbay."

Surprised, Kirk looked up at him.

"Should Berlis link with me, influence me," Spock continued, "McCoy will have to sedate me."

Nodding them toward the turbolift, Kirk agreed. "Let's go."

Spock sat still on the edge of a bed. McCoy monitored his vital signs, occasionally frowning at Kirk, who watched until the silence was finally too unbearable.

"Spock?"

"Yes, Captain?"

"Is it working?"

"No."

McCoy scowled. "What's wrong?"

Eyes opening, Spock nearly frowned himself. "To access those memories, I must strip away more protections than I'd realized."

The captain paced away, frustrated. "Then we can't . . ."

"There is one possibility," Spock offered, stepping to the desk.

"And?" McCoy pushed.

"A stabilizing agent could be added to the process," Spock said, and looked at Kirk.

"A drug?" McCoy asked.

"No, Doctor." Spock didn't move his gaze from Kirk. "A mind."

"You want to mind-meld with me." Kirk turned toward his first officer. There was nothing in the Vulcan's serene expression that seemed deceptive; he trusted Spock, despite all that had happened. Yet Kirk couldn't deny that if Berlis *were* still linked with Spock, this would be the perfect way to neutralize possible interference by the *Enterprise*.

"Why him?" McCoy demanded.

Spock explained to Kirk. "Your resolve helped pull me away from Berlis's link in the first place. The strength of your will, combined with mine, should be enough to allow sufficient mental shields to be dropped." He stood, almost reticent to admit he needed assistance, and yet logic obviously demanded he did. "As you once needed me to help you disbelieve the illusions of the Melcotians," Spock said, "I need you to keep Berlis from reconnecting with my mind."

"Do it." Kirk marched close enough for Spock to reach out and touch his face.

"Jim—what if Berlis . . . what if this is a trap?" McCoy pushed himself between the two of them. "Maybe Spock is still under his influence. What happens if you two meld and Berlis is still there?"

McCoy was merely echoing the concerns Kirk had already considered and dismissed. But Kirk was curious. "What would happen, Spock?"

The Vulcan shook his head. "Unknown."

"Can you assure me he's not in that Vulcan noggin of yours, just waiting for our guard to drop?" McCoy pressed.

"I cannot." Spock turned fully to Kirk and his voice softened. It was the tone he took when discussing private matters. "It *is* a risk, Jim. If I *am* still under Berlis's control, I wouldn't know enough to tell you otherwise. I wouldn't *conceive* otherwise. That is the insidious nature of his power."

With a wave of his hand, Kirk gestured for McCoy to back off and for Spock to proceed. "Let's go."

Moving in closer, Spock placed first one set of fingers on the captain's face, then a second set. "My mind to your mind," Spock said, shutting all other stimuli out. "My thoughts to your thoughts. Our minds are one." Spock moved his fingers from one location to another, pressing on Kirk's face as the captain's eyes glazed. "Two become one . . ."

"Two . . . become one . . ." Kirk repeated, and slowly closed his eyes. "Another mind . . ."

"Yes," Spock said. "It wishes to join." He whispered. "It is a troublesome mind . . ."

"No," Kirk snarled. "It is not allowed."

"It wishes . . ." Spock nearly pleaded.

"No, we can't."

"It wishes . . ." he repeated, his voice uncharacteristically passionate. "It is familiar."

"Request . . ." Kirk said through gritted teeth, "denied!"

"It is lonely, it is searching—" Spock breathed. "He inspires. He encourages. He beseeches us."

"Troubled!" Kirk barked. "Deny him!"

"Yes. Yes, troubled. Oppressive."

"The troublesome mind." Kirk relaxed his tension. "How do we stop it? What is his weakness?"

"Troublesome. Troubled. Initiator," Spock murmured.

"History!" Kirk ordered Spock, or himself, or both. "Search!"

"Many troubled minds. Many destroyed. Many controlled. One . . . gone."

"Exiled." Kirk sighed.

"Exiled. And alone."

"Exiled."

Slowly, Spock pulled his fingers away. Kirk opened his eyes, and the link was broken.

"Thank you, Captain," Spock said.

"A woman." Kirk smiled, but only lightly. He was near exhaustion. "Another troublesome mind." He sighed heavily, pulling in and then letting out a cleansing breath. "Could she still be alive?" He drew a sleeve across his forehead, mopping his brow.

"Well, *I* wasn't in your heads," McCoy groused. "What the devil are you talking about?"

Kirk staggered to McCoy's desk and threw himself into a chair as the doctor began scanning him. "There was another troublesome mind," Kirk said. "Decades ago. Like Berlis, she wasn't discovered until later in life."

"Compared with in utero," Spock interjected. "She was an adolescent."

McCoy nodded as he listened. "Damned Vulcan voodoo," he grumbled as he took a hypo and injected Kirk's arm.

Shocked, Kirk looked up sharply.

"It'll give you energy."

The captain nodded and continued sorting through the results of the meld. "She was weaker than Berlis. She controlled large clusters of people, but eventually her control fell off—dissipated."

"She was separated from her community," Spock said, steepling his fingers in contemplation. "Left isolated for several months, which, itself, proved problematic. It was early in their space exploration phase and her family appealed to have her sent into space."

"Where?" McCoy asked as he began to scan Spock.

"Away," Kirk told him. "There was no heading other than out of the solar system."

"A young girl? Sent alone into space?" McCoy was outraged for her. "Even if she found a habitable world, how would she know how to—well, do anything?"

"She would know anything her people knew, Doctor," Spock said. "Remember, they have no books, no teachers. Their knowledge is entirely shared on a racial level."

McCoy considered that a moment. "Okay, say she's out there. Another of these troublesome minds gets us what, exactly?"

"She was controlled somehow, for a certain amount

of time." Refreshed from the doctor's potion, Kirk stood up. "If we can find out how . . . or—Spock, there was something about two troublesome minds coexisting, do you remember that?"

He nodded. "I do. Ancient. They could not influence one another and wrestled for control of the people for years until one took over."

"When the other died?" McCoy asked. Having finished scanning Spock he prepared another hypo.

"Negative. One was older, and as he aged and weakened, the younger mind was able to assert itself with more vigor." Spock didn't react to the shot.

"We have to find this woman—this other mind," Kirk said.

McCoy placed his kit on the desk, casting it aside as if discounting the whole affair. "It makes no sense, Jim. If she's older, how do we know she'd be strong enough to subvert Berlis?" He turned to the cabinet behind his desk and pulled out a bottle of bourbon and two glasses. "And how do we know she'd not be a worse threat than Berlis? Find her and bring her here, and you could be replacing a benevolent despot with a malevolent one."

Kirk took a glass from McCoy and waited for him to fill it. "We won't know until we find her."

"There were rumors about the direction in which her ship was sent," Spock said.

"Yes." Kirk looked at the filled glass, took only a

small sip, then set it on McCoy's desk. "We'll cross-reference those with our star charts. If we can find her, and if she's alive *and* willing to help us and her people . . ."

"Hell of a lot of *ifs* in there, if you ask me." McCoy took a larger swig from his own glass.

"I didn't," Kirk said, half seriously. At McCoy's sour expression, the captain softened. "Bones, it's all we've got."

"That," McCoy said, mocking the idea with a raised glass, "is the most depressing news of the day."

TWELVE

I'm sorry, Admiral Das, but there is no word from Sa-Gahnesaam." Commander Sheh-Keshemger was not old enough to have been in the last Isitri war, but had heard tales that chilled her, sickened her . . . and now such times were upon her and yet she felt numb. She'd joined the fleet specifically because of those stories, and because her mother, grandmother, and two uncles had also served, defending her planet. Those were only the family members who'd fought in the Isitri wars *and* had survived.

The admiral fussed with several papers on his desk, searching aimlessly for nothing in particular. She knew him well enough to know he was moving simply to move—to have something to do as he contemplated his loss. "Yes," he said. "I understand."

Gently, Sheh pressed on, making sure he truly comprehended. "If they were detaining him, there would be word through diplomatic channels." She reached out a little, then quickly pulled her hand back, unwilling to break protocol. She nervously stroked her beard, as if that were where her hand had been going all along. "We must assume he is lost."

"He trusted them," Das whispered harshly, bitterly. "And I suspect doing so has hastened his ending."

"He was kin to you." She didn't know for certain, but his posture expressed a sense of deep loss. His shoulders were weighed down with sadness.

"He may as well have been." Das stood up and turned toward the port. He looked out at the starscape, perhaps wishing he could see Isitra, and in doing so understand her. "I've known—" He corrected himself. "I *knew* him many years. Since he went into the diplomatic service and I into the military, I thought certainly he would outlive me." He sighed heavily. "I was mistaken."

Sheh lowered her head respectfully. "I grieve with you."

Pivoting back toward the desk, Das sat intently and called up something on his computer screen. "I do not merely grieve, Commander. I intend to get revenge."

Without looking up he asked, "What is our fleet status?"

He was all business again, and somehow that stirred confidence in her. She hoped it wasn't short-lived. "Seventy-three percent, building to seventy-five," she said. "The High Congress suggested keeping one quarter in reserve to protect the homeworld."

Das shook his head. "I will overrule them in this case."

Nervously, Sheh bit the inside of her lip. "You have the authority, of course, Admiral, but—"

"The Isitri fleet is bound to be under the troublesome mind," Das said, still looking at things on his screen rather than at her. "For them to attack our planet he would have to leave the system with his ships. He will not, for that would leave their world open to attack."

The logic was sound. Such a young troublesome mind would not risk sending his fleet out of his sphere of influence so early. Nevertheless, Das's voice seemed desperate. Sheh wondered if the admiral wasn't anxious to take charge of the situation since he'd failed to control the one thing he truly wanted to control: Sa's safety.

"How long before the full fleet is ready?" he asked.

"An additional . . ." she checked. "Seventeen hours, sir."

"Intelligence estimation of the Isitri fleet's readiness?"

"We cannot be sure, without information from Ambassador Sa-Gahnesaam's party—" Sheh caught herself. It was stupid and callous and she'd gotten so into the rhythm of work that she hadn't considered how that might sound. "I'm sorry, Admiral."

He shook his head and motioned for her to continue.

She pulled in a deep steadying breath, then continued. "We estimate less than eleven hours."

Das nodded and gestured for her to leave. "See to the readiness of the remainder of the fleet."

She rose, made it most of the way to the door, and then decided to turn back. She'd always known Das to be decisive, stern even, but rarely impulsive. His judgment felt rash. "If I may, sir, I think you gamble with our lives."

A nod told her nothing. Das could have been dismissing her, or considering what she said. She wasn't sure.

"Perhaps," he said finally, his tone riddled with regret. "But it's a bet I believe we shall win."

"I calculate the odds at eleven hundred to one." Though Spock was flipping switches on his library computer console, his computation had been internal.

Kirk stroked the edge of his chin thoughtfully with his thumb. "Pretty low odds, Mister Spock."

"Higher than the other options given to us by warp-probe telemetry, which are all far more distant." At the punch of a button, one of the screens above him, which displayed a star chart, wavered into a closer view of a solar system. "Sao five-three-three. Within range of the early Isitri warp craft, with two habitable moons and one inner planet."

"The gas giant has *two* M-class moons?" Chekov asked.

With another push of a button the screen changed to show a distant scan of the gas giant and several natural satellites. "One is quite lush, the other somewhat less so," Spock said, "but sensors indicate both support a varied flora-fauna environment."

With her earpiece in place, Uhura gestured to the viewscreen above Spock's console. "And the inner planet?"

"Somewhat less hospitable, but according to probe data, signs of basic civilization. Approximately Class-D."

"You're an Isitri girl," Kirk said, pacing the upper bridge and thinking out loud. "You're thrust into exile by your own people. Where do you go?" He looked around. "Opinions."

"The inner planet," Uhura said confidently.

Chekov scoffed. "This far out? She'd think about survival and go to the moon with the most lush habitat."

But Sulu agreed with Uhura. "I say the inner planet."

When Chekov looked at both Sulu and Uhura as if

they'd lost touch with reality, Uhura explained: "She's alone. If she saw there were signs of civilization, not only would she need people to help her survive physically, but also emotionally."

Kirk agreed. "She was used to touching millions of minds, suddenly stranded alone in space. She'd seek out others." He turned to his first officer. "Spock?"

The Vulcan nodded. "An Isitri mind, begging to contact another soul, would want even a primitive, non-telepathic mind close by."

"Bones?"

The doctor's brows shot up. "If y'all right?" Kirk leveled a serious stare in his direction and McCoy grudgingly offered, "Inner planet."

"I agree." Kirk nodded and turned toward Scotty. "Mister Scott, how are we faring?"

"Warp power's available, sir." Leaning over the engineering console, Scotty checked one last readout. "I can give you warp four."

The captain lowered himself into the command chair and checked the chronometer. At warp four, they'd be cutting it close. But what choice did he have? "Chekov, lay in a course. Sulu, warp factor four."

The Enterprise *is no longer within sensor range of our ships.*

Berlis's jaw quivered. *That is sad. Spock is missed.*

Can you sense him? Chista asked.

Berlis huffed out a frustrated breath. *I cannot. I wish to extend my range.*

Is that possible? another of the council members wondered.

Berlis thought it might be. *If Juah takes his vessel a distance away, and Onro doubles that distance from Zero, and Eklan then triples his—*

There was a clamor of mutual agreement: *Yes, a chain.*

A thought chain from here to First.

We can connect with the colony, and add their sensors to our own.

An early warning system should the Odib attack the colony first. Berlis chuckled at his little pun, and the planet chuckled with him.

Be careful not to travel too far, my friends, he told them. *I cannot bear to be disconnected from any of you.*

Nor we you, came the response, in planetary unison. *Nor we you.*

Enterprise glided majestically toward a brownish-gray planet that revolved around a white-yellow star. "Sao five-three-three gamma," Sulu announced.

"Standard orbit." Usually, finding a new inhabited world was exhilarating. Today Kirk was anxious. McCoy was right—a lot of *ifs* had to fall into the right place for their outlandish plan to work.

"Aye, sir. Standard orbit." Sulu tapped at his console and it beeped responsively. At his command, *Enterprise* slid into orbit.

"Spock?" Kirk restlessly turned to the rail beneath the science station.

"Scanning . . ." Spock peered into his sensor viewer, his hands blindly tapping at buttons and flipping switches. "Mostly arid climate," he reported. "Definite humanoid inhabitants. Global population approximately one hundred seventy million, clustered around small inland lakes, one large inland ocean, and several small rivers. As long-range sensors suggested, no indication of advanced technology."

Kirk couldn't see the Vulcan's face but knew his eyebrow had popped up when he slowly rolled out a contemplative "Interesting . . ."

"What is it, Spock?"

"Refined metal." He turned and looked at Kirk. "Not far from a village."

"A ship?" the captain asked, twisting toward the main viewer and studying the planet below.

"Possibly enough mass, but no power generation."

"A place to start looking." Kirk turned and launched himself toward the turbolift. "We're beaming down," he told McCoy.

The doctor grabbed Kirk's arm and stopped him just before he reached the turbolift doors. "Jim, she could have come here, crashed, and died. Or passed away from illness and otherwise be long dead."

The captain looked at McCoy a long moment, then called to Spock to join them. "Sulu," he said as the turbolift doors opened for them, "take the conn."

THIRTEEN

The hot air assaulted his lungs as soon as they'd materialized. There was only a slight breeze but it was scorching enough to make Kirk instantly feel as if he were in a sauna. McCoy was already dabbing sweat from his brow and Spock . . . well, he looked cool and collected. Even the gentle wind didn't disturb his dark hair.

Consulting his tricorder, Spock pointed at the distance. They'd beamed down behind a bluff that was far enough to hide them from the indigenous populace, but close enough to the source of refined metal they'd scanned.

As they walked, crusted sand crunched under their

boots and Spock continued his scans. "Bearing five degrees, two hundred meters distant."

Quickly they were upon it: an oblong craft, pitted and dented, overgrown with small, dry weeds and crusted with dried sand that had been washed into it by fast-moving floods. It was half buried, and desert life had bloomed in the shade it provided. Some form of cacti or desert flower surrounded it, making it look almost natural. "Various small life-forms inside," Spock said, examining his tricorder. "None humanoid."

"This didn't crash," Kirk said on inspection.

"It's just a shell." McCoy peered inside. "No equipment."

Kirk picked off a leaf that was clinging to the hatchway. "Cannibalized. Stripped." He looked up at Spock. "She survived."

The Vulcan nodded once and turned toward where they knew the humanoid encampment to be. "Individual life signs are indeterminate. We'll have to be closer to the village to differentiate between native and Isitri vitals."

"Let's go." Kirk tossed the leaf to the ground and began marching in the direction Spock indicated. McCoy followed them.

As they trudged along, Kirk couldn't help but wonder if they were tracing the steps of a frightened girl, however many years ago. How long had the trip taken her, and what were her supplies? Was there a sandstorm? Were there natives who instantly killed her on sight? Was this just a wild-goose chase? The answers to those questions weren't in the dust that spread out up the hill. Small brown brush held the dirt against the rise but their journey upward shifted sand beneath them nevertheless. They disturbed the home of small insects, which scurried away from their boots.

Once at the summit, they could look down toward the first indications of a village: rough-hewn huts and signs of life—but no people.

"Where is everyone?" Kirk wondered aloud.

"Jim!" McCoy pointed behind the captain.

Kirk turned to find several diminutive but powerful-looking tribesmen, all in desert protective garb, pointing very sharply carved instruments at their throats.

"I think we found them," McCoy said.

Slowly showing their open hands in a nonaggressive manner, the three Starfleet officers exchanged cautious glances.

Kirk wryly said under his breath, "Take us to your Isitri?"

The indigenous people gestured for them to move, and uttered a few words in their language—but not enough for the universal translator to interpret. Scrambling to their feet, Kirk and his crew shuffled down the front side of the bluff and toward the huts in the distance.

"Captain." Spock's whisper was barely audible. Kirk

glanced toward the direction of Spock's nod and saw two of the natives motioning to each other. It was quick, and for all Kirk knew it could have been the sign language that hunters often used with one another, but he had one of those hunches he sometimes got, and a certain anticipation welled in his chest. Spock must have believed the same, as he was the one to point out the gestures that seemed distinctly Isitri.

As they walked, the smell of water wafted lightly through the warm air. They drew closer to the gathering of huts, and the odor grew stronger. But so did the stench of primitive village life. Kirk wondered how the young Isitri girl would have reacted to the environment her first time. To go from a culture of space flight and advanced technology to one from sub–bronze-age times . . . *jarring* didn't cover it.

Pushed into a small lean-to, Kirk, Spock, and McCoy were left alone, but six guards stood outside the door in a semicircle, all looking in. It was amazingly cool inside the shelter, which may have looked like a simple construction but was certainly not. A reed-like material was interwoven with stronger branches that fortified the walls and roof, and withstood the elements.

When a native's feet shuffled on the dirt outside, Kirk tensed up and looked. Instinctively he readied himself.

The tribesmen parted and allowed a tall, gangly Isitri female entrance to the hut.

Nostrils flaring, Kirk had played the odds—and won. "Spock, can you?"

"Greetings," Spock said, and signed. "We are friends."

"I'm Captain James T. Kirk and we're—"

Eyes bulging in shock, the woman's jaw quivered so hard Kirk thought it might fall off. "You speak my gestural language," she signed back to Spock.

Both voicing and signing, Spock replied. "We have had contact with your people, both on Isitra Zero and Colony First." Kirk noticed that when Spock had signed without speaking he was faster than when he had to gesture and talk at the same time. He wondered if two different parts of the brain were in use: one for spoken language, and one for gestural. Or perhaps it was just difficult using two languages—with two different syntactical structures—at the same time.

"You—" She hesitated, confused. "There is a colony? Where?" Stunned and in shock, she sat awkwardly on the ground, almost stumbling down. Kirk reached out and guided her by the elbow. Once she had her bearings, she gestured for them to join her on the floor. "You are not Odib," she said. "My name is Meshu. But who are you?"

Kirk answered, but she looked at Spock's interpreting. "We're from the United Federation of Planets, and we—"

Tilting her head to one side, she was far more interested in Spock himself than whatever he was signing. "You are a telepath, but your mind is closed."

"Yes," Spock replied.

"Your minds are open," Meshu said of McCoy and Kirk. "But they are simple, quiet."

McCoy scoffed with irony. "I've been thinking the same all day."

"Bones!" Kirk chided, but quickly turned back to Meshu. "We need your help."

"You need my help? You came here looking for me?" She huffed out a breath. "I am exiled."

"Your planet is in danger," Kirk told her, but she huffed again.

"This is my planet," Meshu protested.

Kirk shook his head, then realized that wouldn't be understood and so puffed out his own negative breath. "I mean Isitra Zero."

She looked confused, and also weary. "I don't understand. I can only help destroy my people." She was older than most of the Isitri Kirk had met, or perhaps it was merely the effect of her more difficult life.

"There is a troublesome mind in control of Home Zero," Spock explained. "And the Odib are going to destroy the planet, if they can. If they cannot, your people will annihilate them."

Taking a moment to digest the information, slowly, Meshu began to cry. It was a high-pitched whine and, as a human does, she shed tears.

"I'm sorry," Kirk whispered, and watched Spock sign his apology.

Meshu seemed to gather herself. She wiped away her tears, but licked at her fingers with her pale, narrow tongue, taking back in the moisture and sodium. Probably in keeping with the desert-dweller she'd become. "I was a child when I came here." As she signed, Spock interpreted. "Fourteen revolutions old. These people found me in my ship, close to death. They thought I was a god who had lost her way and hoped to tender favor with me by mending my wounds and nursing me back to health."

McCoy nodded to indicate the tribesmen at the door. "Do they still think you're a god?"

"Some may, who remember my falling from the sky." She smiled sweetly. "But I have explained to them who I am and where I am from. They've learned my sign language and you would be surprised the things we are able to communicate. They're very intelligent. They only lack technological know-how."

"Do you understand their language?" Kirk asked.

"They have no written language, and I cannot hear their sounds," she said.

"You're deaf." McCoy touched his ear.

"I hear very high pitches, but not the vocal range of these beings." She smiled again. "Or you."

Spock signed, "Are you these people's leader?"

"Not intentionally, but I believe they look up to me,"

she admitted. "They protect me, certainly. Perhaps they love me as I love them."

"You radiate an aura of goodwill," Kirk said, not really forming a question. "Like Berlis."

She met Kirk's eyes first questioningly, then with understanding. "I assume Berlis is the troublesome mind."

Kirk told her, "Yes."

Her jaw quivered—probably more a sigh than a shrug. "I cannot change my nature, Captain, so I changed my location."

"Against your will," McCoy said.

Awkwardly, Meshu attempted to nod as she'd seen them do, but it looked more like she was rolling her head on her long neck. "At first. But who was I to argue the right to my will when my presence displaced . . . *usurped* the will of those around me?"

Kirk smiled. "You've gained wisdom."

"Hard won," she said, a light smile thinning her dry lips. "Hard learned."

"Do you miss home?" Spock asked.

This time she both gasped in a breath and attempted the nod. "I miss touching other minds." She was calmer now, and her signing became more natural, less like she was searching for gestures she'd not used in some time. "Toward the end of my journey," Meshu continued, "my craft ran out of enough oxygen for life support. I had to put on a lifesuit. You are spacefarers. Have you ever worn such a device?

"In such a suit you cannot feel the surfaces outside of you, or smell the air, or touch the universe. You are enclosed, cut off. You might move through a room, but it does not possess you fully because you are shut away from it." She looked at Kirk and saw he understood. "You have felt that before." She turned to Spock and met his eyes, but unsure of herself returned to Kirk. "That is how *I* feel, revolution after revolution. I am among beings, as intelligent and wonderful as my own people. But I can never touch them in a natural way."

"But you sense them on some level," Kirk said. "You sensed us, and sent them to meet us."

"You are wise yourself, Captain." She smiled. "I did."

Spock signed, "What did you hope they would find?"

"No one who would hurt them." She turned back to Kirk again. She was looking at Spock only when reading his gestures, or when talking directly to him. Something about him unsettled her, Kirk thought. Was it that his telepathy was tempting to her?

"I enjoy my life, Captain," she said, "within the context of the reality it has become. I enjoy these people and I . . ." She paused, and a realization came over her, hardening her expression. "You think I can stop this Berlis, and wish to take me back to Isitra."

Kirk exchanged glances with both Spock and McCoy, and wondered if perhaps he was the only one who really thought it possible. Whatever the case, he decided a united front seemed more confident. "We do."

"I will not." She stood abruptly. "I will not replace one tyrant with another, especially myself."

Standing up, Kirk put himself between her and the doorway. "You don't think you're in control of these people?" he asked. "What do you call your life here?"

"All I have," she said sadly. "And if I thought I was controlling them, I would end myself."

Kirk felt sorry for her, or did because of her influence. He couldn't really tell which, and on some level it didn't matter, because the emotion was the same.

"If Berlis thought he was controlling his people, he would do the same," Spock countered, signing as he spoke but his voice a thick whisper. "Do you truly know when you're replacing someone's will with your own? I assure you, Berlis does not." Spock stepped closer, boring down on her with his black eyes. "He will bring your people to their doom. But *you* can save them."

Meshu stared at him a long while, then slowly began pushing out breaths, almost a slow-motion hyperventilation. Kirk realized she was essentially shaking her head over and over at the thought of it—at the internal conflict. She collapsed and began to moan, a high-pitched twitter that made Kirk's ears hurt and must have sliced through Spock's skull: He crumpled to the ground.

Meshu's subjects rushed in, frantic, hovering around her at first, then quickly turning their spears toward Kirk's throat.

STOP!

There was no word, for Meshu could not speak, and there was no sound other than the nervous whine through her flat nostrils. But Kirk was certain the command to cease—from her and to all of them—had screamed in his mind.

Everything stopped and all were silent except for Meshu's soft sobs. Isitri sobbing—less through their noses than from inside their chests—had an ebb of complete sadness to it that crashed into Kirk, and likely all of them. McCoy looked startled, the planet natives looked as if they'd received an electrical shock, and Spock . . . Spock was on his knees, curled over, holding his head in his hands.

Kirk rushed to him as McCoy scanned Meshu, and slowly lifted her to her feet.

Lightly putting his hand on Spock's shoulder, Kirk whispered, "Spock?"

The Vulcan looked up. A tear traced down Spock's cheek and there was a fleeting moment of misery in his usually unruffled expression before he instantaneously regained a serene composure.

"What happened?" Kirk asked the Vulcan. He twisted to Meshu. "Are you in his mind?" he yelled.

"Jim, she can't hear you."

"She is not in my mind," Spock said, then signed to Meshu as he spoke. "Your sadness is overwhelming. Why?"

Gasping in and quivering her jaw at the same time, she answered slowly. "Besides the preservation of my life, I'd hoped to gain two things from my exile: the safety of my people, and the assurance that I was usurping no one else's will with my own." She turned to Kirk bitterly, heartbroken. "You've assured me all I have is my own life. An existence that now means nothing."

Kirk grasped her shoulders, holding her frail frame close. Their eyes met. "No," he ground out.

Confused, she looked beyond him to Spock.

The position in which Kirk held her made signing impossible, but he wanted her to listen, not speak. "If you don't want Berlis left in control and you want to save your people, help us. Help them. We won't leave you there. We'll bring you back here."

She pulled out of his grip and began signing vigorously. Kirk looked to Spock to translate but he shook his head. "Too fast." He signed to her, "Slow down, please. I don't understand."

"Icha bilk, Meshda. Icha colimar sithdou zibechna." It was one of the natives, a small, dense young man, whispering in a tone that suggested he was appealing to Meshu in some way. He dropped his spear and was signing to her—and speaking.

"He's telling her not to be distressed," Spock said.

Within moments the universal translator had enough to begin deciphering his language.

"Icha be sad, Meshda," he repeated. "Do not believe we love you for any reason but our *own* love for you."

She lowered her head, her slight shoulders softly heaving with quiet sobs.

"You would not say that," Meshu said, "were I not here."

"We always knew your nature," the tribesman assured her. "You explained it to us." The look in his eyes was that of a son to his mother, and it looked very genuine. "When you were ill with the zezu bite, and asleep with the sickness for many long days and nights, I tended you." He huffed. "Not because you told me to, but because of who you are."

"You don't understand," she said. "Even asleep, my subconscious—"

"I do not care. I am happy with you," he insisted, "and you are happy with me. That is all that matters."

"No," she said, her hands crossed in a blocking motion. "No, you must know your love comes from within and not from without." She turned to Kirk. "*I* must know it."

"Then go," the native said. "Go with them and help

your people." He turned to the captain. "Before you bring her back to us, guarantee without her presence that we still love her. I do not doubt that we will . . . but she must not doubt that our love is genuine."

Kirk nodded, then also gasped to affirm.

Meshu reached out and touched Kirk's arm, pulling him toward her. "What must I do?" she asked. "I will help."

FOURTEEN

H ow is she, Bones?" Kirk had paced anxiously outside the guest quarters waiting for McCoy. McCoy and Spock had both attended Meshu, so the captain didn't want to get in the way even if it meant waiting outside.

"More relaxed now, but still a bit frantic," the doctor said as the door slid closed behind him. "Spock's still in there. I'm not sure how *he* is."

The captain considered replying but decided against it. The truth was that he wasn't sure about Spock himself. He'd insisted to McCoy that he'd know if Berlis had control of the Vulcan again, but would he? Kirk *thought* he would—especially after the mind-meld—but what about Meshu? She had been so agitated, so despondent, that she'd managed to push her emotion through not only to a group of non-telepaths, but also to Spock despite his extensive mental defenses. If she was still in his head—perhaps even *unaware* that she was, and if Spock was oblivious . . . how could Kirk begin to know?

After too long a look at the cabin door, wondering how both Spock and the Isitri woman were doing, Kirk finally turned to face McCoy. "Do you have a medical opinion to convey, Doctor?"

"I do." He straightened with formality, yet managed to keep his skeptical expression. "I'll admit I'm surprised we even found Meshu, but I don't think she's up to pulling Berlis off the top of the totem pole."

Kirk allowed himself a sigh. "She's the only option we have. With Spock's help—"

"And who's going to help *him*?"

The captain leveled his best hard stare at McCoy, but as usual that garnered no result other than somewhat softening the doctor's tone.

"Jim, what's the one thing we've always been able to count on with Spock? His stability. His skill at slicing through the emotion of a matter to give us the raw logic." Was that admiration in McCoy's voice? "I'm not sure that's possible right now. I've never seen him this unsteady." McCoy's worry was evident. "He's struggling to maintain his inner balance."

Few people knew Spock as well as Kirk and McCoy,

yet so much about him was still mysterious even to them. They'd each seen the emotions the science officer kept veiled from others—perhaps even from himself. Spock was well trained at keeping those feelings in check, but being half human meant he was used to having to do so more than a full Vulcan. What remained unclear was how he could control emotions that were not his own.

"How do we help him, Bones?"

McCoy opened his mouth to speak but Kirk cut him off.

"I don't want to hear 'I don't know,' Doctor."

Annoyed but tight-lipped, McCoy looked away as Kirk turned toward the cabin and pushed the chime. The door slid open, he entered, and as it closed again behind him he heard McCoy's faint grumble, "Well, I don't."

Sitting at opposite sides of the small desk, Spock and Meshu were having a discussion in the Isitri sign language. He noticed that both of them didn't really watch each other's gestures, but instead seemed to look into each other's eyes. They obviously caught the signs in the periphery, but facial expression—almost like a mime—had much to do with the method of communication.

Kirk marveled at how fluidly Spock signed, despite having known the language only two days. Kirk also noticed that more gestures had become clearer to him. Whether that was because of his mind-meld with Spock, or simply his exposure to the language, he couldn't be sure.

The two stopped their discussion when Meshu perceived Kirk in the doorway. "Captain," she greeted. She was far more self-composed than she was on the planet and looked up to him in wonder, her round eyes gleaming. "Your ship is beautiful. Spock has been explaining your mission. How wonderful it must be to travel the stars and explore new life."

He couldn't help but smile at her enthusiasm, which jarred him—he couldn't help himself when Berlis was aboard, either. The smile faded from his lips.

"Has Mister Spock had time to brief you on our plan?"

She gasped a "Yes" and looked down at the table, as if embarrassed to criticize. "I don't believe it can work."

The captain looked at Spock.

"Meshu lacks the confidence," the Vulcan said matter-of-factly. "I've explained the extent of Berlis's control."

Beginning to shake nervously, Meshu wrapped her arms around herself. "He's far stronger than I ever was, Captain. I unwittingly manipulated thousands, perhaps hundreds of thousands of people, but billions? It's beyond me. And if his ability is that strong—"

"You touched my mind," Kirk pointed out. "That's

something even Berlis couldn't do." He closed the distance between them, trying to bolster her confidence with his. "I *know* you have this in you." He didn't—not really. But he wanted her to believe it. Could he hide his own uncertainty from a telepath? For that matter, could he do so with someone who used a manual language? His words might say one thing, but could she read some inconsistency in his body language?

"I'll lose myself to him. I can't do this!" Meshu's expression was racked with guilt and fear. One hand clapping into another over and over again, Spock interpreted, "Can't. Can't. Can't."

"Meshu," Spock told her, "we will not force you to do anything you don't wish to do."

"Can't," she said. "Can't." But then she was silent, and as if exhausted, laid her head flat on the desk and closed her eyes.

The bird-like quality of her appearance—of all Isitri—struck Kirk once more. The females were indeed larger than the males but still rather slight. It made Kirk think of them as fragile, breakable.

"There is, of course, the other time concern, Captain," Spock said. "Meshu has confirmed why the Odib fear Isitri's troublesome minds. So long as Berlis lives and remains an influence to his people, the longer the period they can be outside his control before they realize his goals are not theirs."

The implications were just as they had expected.

"How long, Spock?" Kirk asked. "How long before he can send out his fleet?"

"I have no data on which to base a hypothesis," Spock said, and the captain almost wished McCoy was there to ask why the Vulcan couldn't just say "I don't know."

"Does this throw a wrench into our plans?" Kirk tried to massage the knot building in his neck.

Spock shook his head. "We would be ripping Berlis away quickly. The Isitri would return to normal with alacrity." He indicated Meshu with a nod in her direction. "But without her confidence, our plans cannot come to fruition."

Stepping closer, Kirk reached out his hand, wanting to pat Meshu's shoulder to give her reassurance, but the bosun's whistle sounded and he was drawn instead to the small desk viewer.

"Kirk here."

Sulu, sitting in the command chair, appeared on screen. *Approaching the Isitri system, Captain. Scans indicate a change in the distribution of their fleet.*

"On screen." Kirk looked away a quick moment, exchanging a glance with Spock as the screen showed a tactical view.

The muscles in his shoulders instantly tensed. The knot in his neck became Gordian. "Thank you, Mister Sulu. Maintain course. Slow to impulse upon entering the Isitri system."

"Aye, sir."

Kirk thumbed the comm off. "He's put ships around Isitra Zero. Equidistant from one another."

"Interesting," Spock said thoughtfully.

"Would that expand his influence?"

Pausing for consideration, Spock hesitated. "In a sense. Each Isitri mind would provide a link to the next."

"He's building a long chain," Kirk said as he began to pace the small cabin. "Creating a perimeter in which his fleet will have maneuvering room to battle."

"And keep an enemy fleet as far away from the planet as possible," Spock offered.

Suddenly looking up, Meshu reacted to Kirk's pacing, perhaps feeling the vibration of his steps through the deck plates.

With her awake, Kirk decided to rehash one of his fears for her benefit.

"What if Berlis made way for Vulcan, Mister Spock?" Spock was again interpreting their conversation into sign.

"What if he got hold of a race that could telepathically communicate over long distances?" Kirk asked.

Spock didn't hesitate. "He would have an army in his grasp, no matter his distance from them, and no matter the amount of time they were away from him."

"In the case of Vulcan, it would be an army that could cripple the Federation with their inside knowledge," Kirk said. "Our closest allies could helplessly become our most dangerous enemies." Spock paused mid-sign and exchanged a look with his captain. Kirk wasn't talking just about the planet Vulcan, but about his friend. "Could Berlis consider doing something like that?"

"If it meant his own self-preservation," Spock said, pausing only to interpret Kirk's question, "and what he perceives to be the preservation of his planet. If he fears Federation interference, he could already be making such plans."

"He said he found Vulcans fascinating," Kirk recalled, "and hoped to visit your homeworld someday."

Spock rose, and without signing had Meshu wondering what was being said. "Captain, with Meshu having demonstrated the ability to broadcast to human minds as well, Berlis—whose ability is far stronger in general—can surely not be allowed to travel to Vulcan or Earth."

The captain motioned to the Isitri woman who sat at the desk and bewilderedly looked up at them. "I'm not the one you have to convince."

"I remain unconvinced," Sheh-Keshemger told her admiral.

Das dismissed her concern with a shrug and waved her closer to the command chair. "Commander, I am aware of your views," he said in a harsh whisper. "But I command this fleet and I have been charged with protecting our planet from our enemy."

Sheh felt an eyelid twitch. It often did when she was under stress, and she wondered if Das noticed it. Certainly it felt like her entire face was fluttering. His stern expression didn't suggest he had seen it.

With a frown, she accepted that she wasn't in control of the situation, but her duty to question Das was of no less importance.

"Long-range scans now indicate the Isitri fleet has deployed in a heretofore unseen formation. Without knowing more about the reason for this—"

Das cut Sheh off. "The last time we delayed matters, giving them the benefit of the doubt, they launched long-range weapons that disabled our outposts and defense systems." He twirled his hand around, to indicate the universe in general. "Where are those outposts now? We still have not managed to rebuild them, have we? Shall we allow the Isitri to bounce us farther back this time? Perhaps to our stone age?"

Frustrated, Sheh furrowed her brow. They shouldn't waste time discussing the ends on which they already agreed. What she wanted to debate was the tactics, not the goals. "Of course not."

"The longer one of these troublesome minds is in control, the farther their people can leave their influential sphere before beginning to question their purpose." Eyes flashing disgust, and maybe a little fear, Das charred her with a glare. "What is the strength of this particular mind?"

"We are not certain," she admitted.

He nodded as if he'd proven his point. "You see why we must not wait to find out?" He wasn't really asking a question.

"The last ruler spent months in control before venturing out and—" Sheh protested.

"And the one before that mere days." He shook his head and turned toward the viewscreen. "No, this shall not be left to chance."

That was it. The end of the discussion. "Yes, Admiral." Once Das had turned away he'd tuned out any reasoning but his own, and it was time to defer to him. But she couldn't quite leave it anyway. "One question, if I may?"

He nodded very tightly, a quick up-and-down motion—once.

"What if this troublesome mind defeats our fleet and then comes to conquer our world as the rubble of our ships orbits their sun?"

Das still refused to meet her eyes. "We will not allow that to happen," he said.

Relinquishing her position at his side, she bowed her head and retreated for the rear of the command center. "I hope you are right."

"I hope the same, Sheh." His voice, she sensed, did have in it a little doubt.

• • •

Chista told Berlis that the fleet was in a defensive position around the inner star system and was almost in place in the outer system.

Epiltan explained that long-range scans were imperfect, but suggested the Odib were gathering a fleet. It was not unexpected news, but it did sadden him nevertheless.

Berlis wished that the sensor technology of the Isitri was as strong as or stronger than the Odib's. Much to his pleasure, word came instantly from the Akawri province that the minds most adept at engineering were working on such an improved sensor array and it would be built in Akawri's capital city within the hour. Berlis was touched by their support and hard work, and humbled by their dedication. They were equally touched and humbled by his good wishes.

When one of the key ships slipped into place near Colony First, all Istria glowed with pleasure—they were again connected to one another. Colony First rejoiced, mentally embracing Berlis and their extended family. Istria was one, and this pleased Berlis and all the rest.

Soon after, when the new sensor array was brought online, an incredible melancholy washed across the planet: the Odib fleet was on its way to the Isitri system. This wasn't what Berlis wanted. It wasn't what anyone wanted. Welling up with emotion, Berlis suggested Colony First might come under attack before Zero Home.

Golo, happy to be connected to Berlis again but distressed at learning the Odib were ready to attack, assured his people that the civilian craft of the colony could quickly be converted to military fighters. Berlis feared for them nevertheless, but was inspired by their commitment, and all of Isitra felt the same.

FIFTEEN

"Can't, can't, can't." It was Spock's voice, but Meshu's words.

Was it personal fears? She'd lived a difficult life, and hadn't struck Kirk as weak, but she was adamant that even with Spock's help the plan would not work.

"What scares you?" Kirk asked, glad they'd decided to stay in the cabin's intimate setting rather than going to sickbay as McCoy had suggested. "The doctor will monitor the meld. You'll both be fine."

"Berlis is too strong," she said, while Spock interpreted.

"I can teach you disciplines," the Vulcan told her. "You will be safe." There was a certain amount of emoting necessary for gestural language, and Kirk noticed

Spock's voice was also more expressive when he spoke as he signed.

"I can't," Meshu replied. "I won't."

"Why?" Kirk balled his fists and put them on the desk as he leaned down. "Meshu—*why*?"

McCoy took a half step toward her, but was still behind the captain. "Is it because you believe you *can* steal control from Berlis?"

Spock's brow rose in surprise. McCoy had it. When Spock interpreted for her, Meshu gasped in an affirmative breath.

She looked into Kirk's eyes and signed slowly but passionately to him. "I have not touched a mind for many years, until distress compelled me to touch yours," she told them, then put her head to one side, resting it on her own shoulder.

She was embarrassed, Kirk decided, and her body language was the equivalent of a human looking down dejectedly. "It was a difficult moment," Kirk said. "We understand."

"You cannot appreciate the feeling," Meshu huffed at him, then looked up at Spock. "You may. I am not sure."

"You're barking up the wrong Vulcan if you think *he* understands a feeling," McCoy sniggered.

Spock signed the insult, and Meshu looked harshly at McCoy. He shrugged apologetically.

"Explain it to us," Kirk said after he cast his own sideways glance at McCoy.

Meshu gasped that she would, but hugged herself, placing her arms around her sides for an extended time. Her eyes closed; it almost looked as if she were sleeping. Suddenly, her eyes opened and she began gesturing. "There was a young boy in my adopted village who would visit the cliffs where he knew he should not play. Children do childish things, and Cheshu's parents became worried when he did not return home one evening." Her gaze became suddenly distant as she pulled up an old, perhaps painful memory. "We searched and searched and could not find him until the next night. He'd fallen, and a large boulder had slid from the mountain above and pinned his left arm and left leg. He was ill, in shock, and when we freed him the nurses could not save his arm or leg—the bones were crushed."

McCoy shifted his weight from one leg to the other. Kirk knew he wanted to somehow propel himself back in time and to that planet to help the boy. Such was the size of the doctor's heart.

"We removed what was left of them, cauterized the wounds, and though it took weeks, he survived the fever," Meshu continued. "His foot would always itch, he said, even though it was no longer there, and his hand would reach for things, for people, and of course, touch nothing."

Leaning down, McCoy gently patted Meshu on the shoulder. "Phantom pain isn't uncommon."

She glanced at him, accepted his wisdom with an inclined head, then continued: "Then I'm sure the dreams are also common. Every night, eyes closed, he possessed two arms and two legs. He would run, he would play . . ." She smiled sweetly, sadly. "He would even dream of walking the cliffs again." Her jaw quivered. "Every morning came the shock that things were not as he had hoped. He spiraled into depression. With time he came to accept his life. Children grow up and the people of my village are nothing if not adaptable." Her eyes met Kirk's. "But I understood his loss."

"The link with your people," Kirk said.

"The link with *any* people," she signed with a gasp. "I tasted that feeling again, with you, for the first time in years, and only for a brief moment." She quivered her jaw again, longer this time: a heavy sigh. "I used to dream of it every night. I used to crave it every waking moment. As I grew older I dreamed of it less . . . but I would wake up in the night and my first thought would be to remind myself of the depth of my loss." She looked at Spock now, sensing in him a kindred spirit. "There are nights, after many years, that I don't think about it at all. But there are also nights I do."

"Are you afraid I won't be able to control your access to my mind after the meld?" Spock asked. "That I will be unable to break the bond with you?"

"I haven't thought about that," she admitted. "I fear that once I have relinked with my people, I shall never wish to let them go. And knowing how the Isitri minds work, they will assure me I should stay."

"We'll protect you," Kirk offered.

"Why wouldn't I stop you from trying, as Berlis surely will?" She huffed twice—the second one was long and from deep within, almost an actual sigh.

"I have confidence in you," Kirk told her with a shake of his head. "If you can ask this question now, I don't believe you'd lack such conscience and keep an entire planet enslaved."

"Captain, were I to take your arm and leg, or your eyes, or your . . . whatever it is you hold most dear—"

My ship, Kirk thought, but simply clamped his jaw tightly.

"I won't ask what you might do to regain whatever you could not bear to lose. But I'll ask you what you would do to keep it, once finding it again." Her expression—or perhaps her mind—broadcast such sorrow that Kirk almost flinched. "You could teach me how to control Berlis and therefore all Isitri. You could teach me to release them and I could return to exile." Her bulbous eyes glistened with tears. "What if I don't wish to?"

"Is that what you want?" McCoy asked.

"No. But it may be too within my nature to avoid it." Meshu rolled her head around, wiping each eye on a respective shoulder.

Spock turned to Kirk and didn't interpret for Meshu. "If I may, Captain, perhaps I can reassure her."

With a nod, Kirk turned for the door and motioned McCoy to go with him. "Do what you can, Spock."

He and McCoy silently made their way to the turbolift and didn't speak until the doors slid closed.

"What now?" the doctor asked.

Kirk grabbed the control handle but didn't activate the turbolift. He stifled a sigh but allowed himself a little shrug. "I need to buy the Isitri some time."

"How?"

"I'm thinking." He twisted the handle. "Bridge," he ordered.

"Say you buy some time. Then what?" The doctor crossed his arms and motioned his head downward to indicate Meshu. "She *doesn't* want to do this."

"Spock will convince her," Kirk assured McCoy, and tried to assure himself as well.

"She fears Berlis—fears *becoming* him," McCoy said. "Maybe there's some wisdom in that."

"You don't feel sorry for her?" Kirk asked.

"I do. But you and I both felt Chista's fear. Meshu was exiled for what she is, and now Chista has fallen into the exact situation he had hoped to avoid."

"And it is my fault." Kirk pulled in a deep, decisive

breath. "I've got to do something to stop the Odib."

"You can't hold off an entire fleet."

The turbolift doors opened onto the bridge and Kirk stepped out as if ejected. "Maybe I can—with an appeal."

McCoy followed Kirk to the command chair as Sulu slipped back to the helm.

"Uhura." The captain lowered himself into his seat. "Try to raise the Odib homeworld."

She nodded and dabbed at her board. "Aye, sir."

"And if they don't take kindly to you asking nicely?" McCoy frowned.

"I don't know, Bones," Kirk said quietly. "I'm out of rabbits to pull out of my hat."

"Huh," the doctor scoffed. "May you be blessed with another hat."

"Who?" Das-Dosiame's eyes narrowed and he looked from Sheh to the tactical screen. "From what ship?"

"Jamesty-kirk, captain of the *U.S.S. Enterprise.* United Federation of Planets?"

"Generic enough name." Das shrugged as he rose and moved to the scanning station. "Can you get a location fix?"

The sensor operator shook his head. "The signal originates from the Isitri system, or near it, Admiral."

"Command is recommending we speak with them, Admiral," Sheh said.

"United Federation of Planets," Das grumbled as he returned to his command chair. "Might as well call themselves the League of Beings." He motioned to the communications officer. "I will talk to them myself."

"I have an Admiral Das, sir." Uhura's right hand hovered over the button that would place the transmission on the main viewer.

Kirk nodded. "On screen."

The starscape washed away and a large man with a bald head and long reddish-black beard filled the screen. *"Who are you?"* Das rumbled.

"Captain James T. Kirk, representing—"

"I know that much. Tell me why you're in this area."

Direct and to the point. Kirk liked that, and explained from the beginning: about the distress call, about Berlis and his effect on Spock, about the shuttle incident and his talk with Chista, all of it. Admiral Das listened quietly and intently, occasionally looking at the woman—also bald and bearded—who stood to his left.

"They know you're coming," Kirk said. "They're preparing for your fleet right now."

"We understand that," Das said. *"We are also prepared."* He leaned down on an elbow and stroked his beard, and appeared to contemplate Kirk. *"What is the purpose of this discussion, Captain? Are you asking to join us, or warning us off?"*

"Neither." *Or both,* Kirk thought. "Admiral, I understand the concerns of your people—"

"No, I don't think you do, Captain." Das stood dramatically and while it was difficult to know for certain because there was nothing with which Kirk could compare the man's height, he looked to stand close to two and a quarter meters tall. His tunic was long in the back like a cloak, and short in front, like a shirt, and as he marched forward it flourished behind.

"You're right," Kirk admitted. "I can't claim to know all the details of your history with the Isitri. But grant me that I've had a crash course since meeting Berlis."

Das nodded unenthusiastically. *"Are you attempting to make an appeal for the Isitri? Asking us not to attack? Because we see your signal originates within their system. What would guarantee me that I'm not speaking to the troublesome mind right now?"*

Pursing his lips, Kirk realized he'd not thought of that when he considered contacting the Odib. Could he suggest Das trust him on his word? If the situation were reversed, Kirk certainly wouldn't trust Das.

Mustering a little of his own drama, Kirk stood and took a step toward the main viewer. "I don't know how to convince you. All I can tell you is that we're trying to save two planets here, and two peoples—"

"That is where we differ, Captain," Das said harshly. *"I am working to save but one."*

"I . . ." Kirk chewed on his inner lip a moment and

debated being this honest with an alien admiral about to go to war. "I feel responsible for this situation," Kirk admitted.

"That makes you perceptive," Das replied dryly. *"But it doesn't convince me there's an alternate course of action."*

"Give me twelve hours," Kirk pleaded for the Isitri, but Das was already shaking his head. "Twelve hours, and if I can't remove Berlis from the equation—"

"This does nothing, Captain Jamesty, but allow them to shore up defenses—and offenses."

"Or it defuses the problem entirely." Kirk took another step toward the viewer and hoped he was looking more imposing to the Odib admiral. "I'll make you a deal, Das. Whether I'm successful—or not—you get a constant telemetry from our sensors: an inside look into this system." He was considering it, Kirk could tell, so he sweetened the pot to put the deal to bed. "I can rid you of Berlis without a life being lost."

"Lives *have been* lost," Das barked.

Kirk nodded and tilted his head down. "We can avoid losing more," he said, neck still tilted down, but eyes burning into Das's.

Das looked to someone off-screen, and the main viewer abruptly went black.

"I don't trust him," Sheh said.

The admiral sighed and returned to the command chair. "Nor do I."

Gesturing to the viewscreen as if Kirk still filled it, Sheh asked, "If we can't trust him, how could we trust his sensor data?"

Quietly, Das considered her question. He sat as if mentally reckoning a long, complicated mathematical formula. "Do we need to? We could use the signal as a carrier for our own sensor telemetry."

With a smile, Sheh showed her admiration for the idea. "Yes, we could. It wouldn't be indicative of much—the detail would be minimal."

Das nodded. "But it would confirm Kirk was sending us the actual data."

"It would," Commander Sheh agreed. "And twelve hours would allow us to bring another three light cruisers online. I'd feel better if we left some protection here."

"Twelve hours." Das nodded and had made his decision. "But I want something else riding Kirk's telemetry." He turned to the crewman at the sensor station. "Get as much information on his vessel as possible. If his ship falls under the troublesome mind's control, it may be necessary to destroy it."

Once he and Kirk were back in the turbolift, the doctor spoke candidly with admiration. "I didn't expect him to accept your terms." McCoy shook his head, releasing a half chuckle. "But twelve hours isn't a long time, Jim. And if Meshu won't help . . ."

"Spock will convince her," Kirk insisted.

The doctor grunted skeptically. "And what if Spock is still connected to Berlis?" The captain opened his mouth to speak but McCoy pressed on. "I *know* you don't think so, but for the sake of argument what if he is, Jim? Berlis would know all about the whole idea. He could be preparing for it right now."

Kirk hadn't considered that, and McCoy wasn't seeing the full ramifications if it were true. "If so, it's worse than that." He twisted the turbolift handle again, speeding them up. "If Berlis is still linked to Spock, what happens when he and Meshu mind-meld?"

By the time they got to the guest quarters and the door opened, Kirk and McCoy found both of Spock's hands pressing into Meshu's face and forehead. "Our minds are one."

SIXTEEN

pock, what have you done?" McCoy rushed to
Meshu's side.

The Vulcan sat back as if at afternoon tea and
steepled his fingers across his chest. "Meshu lacked the
confidence to withstand not only Berlis, but also her
own inner desires. Only through a mind-meld could I
lend her my strength."

"You were supposed to wait, so I could monitor . . .
How do you know she won't give you *her* weakness?"
McCoy countered pointedly.

"She could have," Spock said, "but she did not."

Meshu gasped her affirmation. "*Now* I can do this,
Captain. *We* can do this." She did seem bolstered—
calmer.

"Spock?" Kirk studied his first officer's expression. If Meshu had merely transferred her vulnerabilities to Spock, it didn't show. But would it be so obvious?

"She has the capability," the Vulcan said matter-of-factly.

With a nod, Kirk accepted that.

"You're going through with this?" McCoy stepped closer to Kirk, getting in his personal space. "Jim, this isn't a decision you can make with your gut! Billions of lives are at stake." The doctor waved at Spock. "Tell him. Tell him that, for all you know, Berlis might still be connected to you."

"The doctor is correct," Spock said. "I wouldn't know if Berlis has broken through my protections."

"But I would, Captain." Meshu placed both palms on her own head and then turned them into fists. Kirk recognized the sign as "holding knowledge" and understood, in context, she was saying "I know."

Of course, if Berlis were now directing both Spock *and* Meshu, all this could be a deception.

"For years I've felt the depths of loneliness unlike any you can imagine," Meshu continued while Spock interpreted. "My one mind, unaccompanied by the billions of voices it should naturally hear . . . I cannot relate the profundity in any language. I will admit that it is good to link with another mind—especially with someone like Mister Spock, who has a most interesting and unusual intellect. But I would know if a mind not his was also in the link. There is not."

If memory served, Meshu described Spock's mind in much the same way Berlis did. Was that a clue? Kirk didn't think so. He believed Meshu was sincere.

"I believe her," Kirk said finally, examining Meshu's face while Spock interpreted. The Isitri woman gasped a confident breath and the captain turned to McCoy. "Good enough for you?"

"Does it matter if it's not?" the doctor asked.

"Not really."

"You're taking her word for it, but if Berlis is in Spock's head, and now also in Meshu's, you just asked Berlis to assure you everything was okay." McCoy made the same point Kirk had considered and discounted.

"If he were linked with Spock, his goals would be achieved, and so he would have no reason to lie," Meshu said.

Kirk smirked. "Logical, Bones."

With a sigh, McCoy crossed his arms and grumbled, "Like one of him isn't more than enough."

The smile faded from his lips and Kirk turned to Spock. "Now we just have to get to Berlis."

"That will not be easy," Spock said.

"We have less than twelve hours." Kirk looked at Meshu. "Any advice?"

"I do not know Berlis, other than through Spock," she said, and noticed McCoy's eyes widened.

"Through what I've told her, Doctor," Spock assured McCoy.

"Right." McCoy didn't seem certain and Kirk hoped it was true.

"Gentlemen, and lady . . ." Kirk gestured toward the door. "It's time to make our move."

Once on the bridge, Meshu marveled at the array of technology before her. Kirk took some pride that it astounded her so, as if he'd built *Enterprise* with his own bare hands. "A little more advanced than the craft you've used."

Almost breathless, Meshu gasped, taking in a large gulp of air.

They all followed Spock to his station where he quickly flipped switches and coordinated data. When he turned back toward the captain, McCoy, and Meshu, Kirk nodded toward the sensor scan results showing on the viewscreen above the science station. "Tactical assessment."

"It would appear Colony First is working in synchronization with Isitra Zero." Spock pointed to a line of ships on the system map. "Here, and along this route. Berlis has deployed vessels that have allowed him to create a chain all the way to the colony."

"To what end?" McCoy asked.

Alert lights began to flash on the helm and a Klaxon

sounded. Kirk pivoted toward the lower bridge. "Contact?"

Chekov poked at his console and shrugged. Brow crinkled, he looked back at the captain. "I—I think we're being scanned."

"Fascinating." Spock bent over his scanner and in a short moment straightened up, one brow jutting up. "Both the colony and Isitra Zero are scanning us."

"That's triggering deflector screens?" Kirk peered over Spock toward the report coming up on the second screen above the Vulcan.

"The intensity of their scan is disruptive." Spock nodded and motioned to the power output.

"Since when are their sensors that strong?" McCoy asked.

"They were not," Spock said, just a touch of concern layering his voice, "twelve hours ago."

"How is that possible?" Uhura asked.

A ball of tension knotted in Kirk's back, and another was forming in his stomach. "Berlis can direct an entire population to a single goal."

"He'll see the Odib coming," McCoy said.

Kirk nodded and paced the bridge. "Why would he need such strong sensors?"

"A long-range targeting device?" Sulu offered.

"Possibly," Spock said.

"He *needed* the colony." Kirk turned back to Spock. "Why?"

"Scanning." Bowed again over his sensor cowl, the Vulcan remained there a long time before standing straight and twisting to the captain. "Reading an unusual power signature." He'd neglected to sign the last sentence, and Meshu looked at each of them, confused.

"Full power to shields," Kirk ordered.

Scotty punched at the engineering controls. "Full shields, aye."

As if smacked by a giant electrical fist, *Enterprise* ignited in sparks. Consoles blasted smoke and circuits sizzled above them.

The lights flickered, and dimmed.

Sheh's sensor officer shook his head and repeatedly tapped at his board. "Confirmed. Disruption in the data stream."

"Have we lost telemetry?" Sheh asked.

"Only a momentary fluctuation, but the data is garbled."

"A trick?" She twisted toward communications. "How is our carrier? Are we pulling any of our own data?"

"We are," came the reply.

She stepped to Das's side. "I feared our subterfuge was discovered. It's intact," she said, "but should we risk irritating this Federation?"

Das shrugged and seemed more concerned with why the stream was suddenly garbled. He rose and marched toward the sensor station. "Divert power to computers, Lieutenant. Enhance the data."

The lieutenant poked and prodded his console, moving data to the touch screen with his fingertips. "The Isitri colony is firing on *Enterprise*."

Das looked at the information and watched the simulation based on the data. The moon that housed the Isitri colony fired on the Federation ship a second time.

"Again!" the sensor lieutenant called out.

Sweeping back toward the command chair, Das growled at the helm. "Make way for the Isitri system."

"We gave our word to them—" Sheh protested.

"Dead men hold no grievance." Admiral Das folded himself into the command chair. Disillusioned, he shook his head. "If they're still alive when we arrive, we will defend them. If dead, we will avenge them."

Golo reached out to Berlis and informed him *Enterprise* had been hit by the new weapon. There was disappointment in that fact. They'd hoped Captain Kirk would not interfere further; while Berlis owed Kirk his life, *Enterprise* couldn't be allowed to side with the Odib.

When the targeting scanners suggested there was a transmission broadcast from *Enterprise* to the Odib system, Berlis regretted his next suggestion: Disable the Federation vessel; if necessary, destroy it.

An intense debate followed instantly: Which was the best course of action? Berlis appreciated Spock and had learned much from him, but was he worth saving if it meant keeping the *Enterprise* a threat? Perhaps.

All involved asked Berlis for his opinion, since he knew Spock best and also knew Kirk. Should *Enterprise* be destroyed?

The grief was overwhelming for him—for all Isitra—because the conclusion was *yes. Enterprise,* by helping the Odib, had chosen to betray their friendship. Sadly, it would be their undoing.

"Evasive!" Kirk ordered, and the ship turned so that neither the planet nor moon was on the main viewer. The vessel wobbled under another blast that appeared electrical in nature, zapping circuits from every system. So much damage, so many small pops and explosions—were the deflectors down? "Shields?"

"Shields unaffected, Captain," Chekov reported.

"Wide scatter beam—" Spock's voice was calm and unruffled. "They're tracking us closely."

"Doctor, casualties in sickbay," Uhura told McCoy.

"On my way," he said, and headed for the turbolift.

The bosun's whistle sounded and Kirk jammed down on the comm button.

"Scott to bridge!"

"Yes, Mister Scott."

"We've got an overload in the mains, sir! Engines are off line!"

"Auxiliary power to thrusters," Kirk ordered, and thumbed the button off. But the command was a futile one—thrusters wouldn't provide an escape. "Spock!"

"Damage to most major circuits—inertial dampeners, coolant systems . . ." The Vulcan turned to meet Kirk's eyes. "It's a sensor weapon. Shields cannot block the signal."

They'd encountered sensors before that had been disruptive when scanning, but this was ingenious. It was becoming clearer why the Odib so feared the Isitri. To design—and implement—an entirely new weapon in a matter of hours was chilling.

"We need to get out of here," Kirk said and got back on the comm. "Bridge to engineering. We need warp—"

Booooom! An explosion rumbled somewhere from below.

Scotty's voice crackled from the speaker, peppered with static and sparks. *"I can only keep rerouting circuits so long, sir. As long as they're still training that beam on us—"*

"Torpedoes?" Kirk looked to DeSalle at the engineering station.

He shook his head. "Circuits are cooked, Captain."

Thinking only a short moment, Kirk motioned forward. "Come about. Sulu, take us into the planet."

"Coming about, aye." Sulu twisted with the ship as he steered it toward the gas giant.

"Batten for atmosphere," Kirk ordered and a flurry of crosstalk began across the bridge.

"Rerouting dampeners."

"Confirmed."

"Interconnects braced!"

"Verify."

"All decks, aye."

Another flood of sensor energy cascaded across the ship, making her quake again.

"Thruster circuits damaged," DeSalle called.

Sulu struck at his console. "Bypassing!"

"Spiral us in," Kirk ordered, and Sulu turned back in shock.

"Sir?"

The captain pointed at the helm and Sulu instantly followed the order as Kirk explained. "I want us to look as if we are out of control."

"Aye, sir." Sulu nodded tightly and played with the controls, making his powered descent look rough and random.

Enterprise dove down awkwardly on a haphazard course. The atmosphere first blew out of their way, but the deeper they trod, the more it crushed in on them, making the hull creak under the pressure.

"The atmosphere is dissipating the beam," Spock reported. "It's working."

Kirk nodded. "Reduce forward shields. I want a little flare."

Providing an elegant show, *Enterprise* was burning up in the gas giant's stratosphere.

"Put as much distance between us and the colony as possible," Kirk ordered, his neck beginning to unknot.

"Out of range in ten seconds," Spock called.

The attacks stopped.

Jumping to the upper deck, Kirk nodded approvingly at his own plan. "They'll think we spun in and were crushed by the atmosphere." He tried to smile encouragingly at Meshu, whom he'd forgotten was on the bridge. The slight woman was sitting in the alternate science station chair, long fingers curled around the underside of the seat—holding on for dear life. "Damage report, Mister Spock."

"Several circuits are on bypass." The Vulcan flipped a switch and brought the screen above them to life. An internal dorsal view of *Enterprise* appeared. Red dots indicated a bypassed or downed circuit.

"The ship has measles," Kirk said wryly.

Spock nodded as if Kirk had made a helpful comment. "Some backup circuits are down as well. Sensors are hampered. Warp and impulse are offline, and external communications are down."

"Communications and sensors," Kirk groaned. "The Odib will believe we've backed out of our deal."

"Or that we've been destroyed."

The captain looked at Uhura. "Tell Mister Scott I

want priority on warp, weapons, and inertial dampener circuits."

"Aye, sir."

Kirk shook his head and slid a thumb along his jaw. He looked at Spock. "Getting you and Meshu to Isitra Zero just got that much harder."

Sheh-Keshemger hung her head when the last bits of information rolled across her screen. She loaded the report on a tablet and took it to the admiral.

He glanced at the screen and handed it back to her without a word.

"The last bits of telemetry indicated *Enterprise* was on a desperate, out-of-control course into the gas giant."

"I read it, Sheh."

"Then you read my report on the *Enterprise* itself. Five times larger than our biggest cruiser; their deflectors so sophisticated we can't even rate them; their engines are estimated at three warp factors faster than ours."

Das stroked his beard absentmindedly, as if thinking about more important things. "We obviously won't be doing battle with the *Enterprise,* Commander."

"No," she said. "Just with those who scuttled her in a matter of minutes."

He met her bitter gaze with one of his own. "What would you have us do? You know the history as well as anyone. What's the one trait all their troublesome minds have had in common?"

Sheh needn't think about her answer. "Paranoia."

"*Extreme* paranoia." Das crossed his legs and looked at the starscape that flew past on the main screen. "And tremendous strides made in technology."

"Thanks to our espionage unit, our own technology has been greatly served as well," Sheh pointed out.

Das grimaced. "At the cost of how many lives?"

A heavy sigh escaped Sheh's chest. Das had put the entire Odib fleet on a course that could easily lead to total disaster. "I'm not advocating that we refuse to defend ourselves, Admiral. But neither should we hasten our destruction by pitting our forces against an unstoppable foe."

"The more time passes," Das told her, "the more unstoppable they become." He shook his head adamantly. "We are on an inexorable path, Commander. Captain Kirk wished to delay it twelve hours—and he is dead. Do you honestly suggest we wait and tempt the same fate?"

SEVENTEEN

James Kirk, as the captain of a starship, felt it was his duty to know every station aboard the *Enterprise*. It was his calling to know, and he took it seriously. While that didn't mean he knew the finer details of everyone's job better than they did, if needed he *could* work the ship as any other crewman would. Today, he needed to.

That wasn't quite correct. He *wanted* to. He knew what must be done, and now just needed to repair the tools that would make it possible. If he had not taken a hand in doing the maintenance himself, he'd be sitting—waiting—and that would have been unbearable.

Instead he was helping Scotty plan circuit reroutes and fail overs that would hopefully be better shielded from the new sensor weapon the Isitri had developed.

"Here?" Kirk asked his chief engineer, pointing to the diagram on the clipboard. "No, here," he corrected himself.

Scotty nodded with admiration. "Aye, it should work."

Grabbing a Jefferies tube handrail, Kirk pushed himself up toward the access panel they needed to bypass. "Mister Scott, you almost sound surprised that I know what I'm doing."

The Scotsman scoffed. "You're the only captain in the fleet I'd let touch his own ship, sir." He handed Kirk up the laser probe he needed. "Gettin' your hands dirty now and again clears the brain, doesn't it?"

There *was* something about being in the guts of his ship that contented James Kirk. Like he was a part of her, and she him. He didn't let his mind linger on such a thought, merely accepted the feeling of security as if it were part of the vibration of the bulkheads and deck plates.

Meshu made him wonder what he might do to get back his ship if he'd ever lost it. It was a question he couldn't answer . . . because he honestly wasn't sure.

Would he let hundreds die to save his ship? Thousands? Millions?

It wasn't a proper mathematical equation because the unknown quantity was always, "What hangs in the balance?"

Kirk had asked his first officer to continue working with Meshu, to teach her the finer points of the Vulcan mental disciplines she would need, partly because the captain didn't want to think about some of the trickier aspects of his own plan. Most of all, Kirk didn't want Spock trying to teach the same mental restraints to Berlis.

He assured the Vulcan that Meshu could better teach Berlis because they were both Isitri, but in truth he was more anxious about Spock losing himself to Berlis yet again.

As Kirk reached down the Jefferies tube and exchanged the laser probe for a conduit sealer, he wondered how much Berlis knew about his ship from his short time with Spock. Was it enough that all this crosscircuiting and shielding was worthless? Would Berlis be anticipating this move and directing an entire planet to find a way to overcome it?

How could Kirk defeat billions of people all acting in unison against him?

Weaving one circuit into another, Kirk looked down to see Scotty's form had been replaced by McCoy's.

"They said I'd find you here."

"And you did," Kirk said as he continued working.

The doctor nodded up the corridor, probably to the next access panel where Kirk knew his engineer had needed to complete his part of the bypass. "Not enough to do your own job, you have to do Scotty's?"

Kirk shrugged, but he was probably at too odd an angle for McCoy to notice. "We need all hands to complete this work before the Odib get here."

"They said they'd wait twelve hours."

"They agreed to terms that then became moot when we were attacked and lost the ability to hold up our end of the bargain," Kirk explained.

"Why not trust them to wait anyway?"

"Because *I* wouldn't wait. Waiting isn't smart." Stretching a long cable between two relays that weren't really designed to be connected, Kirk marveled at how technology could be manipulated beyond its intended purpose. "How many hours did it take the Isitri to come up with an entirely new weapon—not just on a drawing board but also building an actual successfully operational model?" he asked McCoy as he worked.

"Not long," the doctor grumbled.

Scotty popped his head in front of McCoy and called up the tube. "Another ten minutes for main engine power, sir. I don't like the way some of those coolant systems look."

Pushing himself down and onto the deck, Kirk nodded. "Very good, Mister Scott."

"Full sensors can be brought back online," Scotty said as he marched purposefully up the corridor, toward main engineering.

"We'll be able to see again," Kirk said.

McCoy gestured to the Jefferies tube. "That means you're done here?"

No, it meant he had something more to do than wait. "I'm just getting started."

"Communications status?" The doctor in tow, Kirk strode from the turbolift to Uhura's station.

"Subspace transceiver circuits are fully bypassed, sir." She looked up at him. "Continuing subspace silence, per your order."

"Maintain," Kirk said. "And call Mister Spock to the bridge, please."

"Aye, sir."

"Subspace silence?" McCoy asked as Kirk retired to the command chair.

"We made it look like we lost control and were crushed in the atmosphere," Kirk explained. "They'd never find wreckage even if they took the time to look. If they assume we're dead, that gives us an advantage."

The doctor stepped down to the lower bridge and took his normal position at the left side of the command chair. "Why would they assume that?"

"Because Berlis is naïve." Kirk reached back and tried to massage a tight muscle out of the back of his neck. "Chista pointed out how young he was. Being in command of anything—a colony, ship, fleet, or planet—it requires a certain amount of experience."

"But Chista wasn't inexperienced," McCoy pointed out. "There'll be plenty of advisers helping him."

"You know what a B-29 is, Bones?"

"Riboflavin and folic acid?"

Kirk's eyes squinted quizzically, his brows knitting.

"Now you know how I feel," McCoy said wryly.

"It's an airplane." Kirk smirked. "A bomber used by the United States in the Second World War. Stalin . . . " He paused, seeing if the doctor remembered his history. "Stalin?"

McCoy smiled mockingly. "Stalin I'm familiar with, thank you."

The captain swallowed a small chuckle. "Even though Soviet Russia fought on the side of the Allies, political tensions were high. The Americans refused to give plans for the bomber to Stalin's air force, and American pilots were warned not to land in Soviet territory—"

"Even in case of an emergency?" McCoy asked.

"Three B-29s had to land under mechanical duress and while Stalin shipped the crews back home—"

The doctor nodded his understanding. "He kept the ships."

"Planes," Kirk corrected. "Yes." He glanced around and noticed Sulu and DeSalle were both listening. Uhura surely was as well.

"You got a point somewhere in here about the Isitri or Berlis?" McCoy asked.

Ignoring the attitude, Kirk pressed on. "Stalin ordered his people to reverse engineer the stolen bombers. Part by part, they copied the planes, until they could build a prototype. Stalin issued orders that the B-29 was to be copied precisely—in all ways—right down to the colors she was painted inside the bomb bay." The captain waved a finger as if Stalin had merely chided his underlings. "No deviation would be tolerated, and the head of the program was also in charge of the secret police." Kirk swiped his thumb across his own throat.

"How convenient."

"He ruled through terror and oppression," Kirk said. "Which . . . worked. They got an exact duplicate of a B-29. But—"

"Here it comes," McCoy said with a good-natured smile.

"Including all her flaws." Kirk's eyebrows shot up at the punchline. "No design is perfect and the American bomber had its share. In reverse engineering it, the Soviet scientists saw these flaws, but were afraid to deviate from their orders to create an *exact* duplicate."

It dawned on McCoy how this related to their present situation. "Berlis doesn't have advisers," he said. "He has followers."

Kirk nodded. "He might not enslave through terror, and his people don't even feel enslaved. But they are. Stalin's people were afraid of defying his will. Berlis's people don't have a will other than his."

A chilling fact, and the dread was evident on the good doctor's face and on Kirk's as well. As the captain turned toward Uhura, he found the same dismay on her face.

"Mister Spock is on his way, sir," she said, her voice unsettled.

Kirk nodded and gave her an encouraging nod and a touch of a smile before heading toward Chekov who was under Spock's station. The young ensign was helping a red-jumpsuited technician with console reroutes. The Isitri weapon could be countered at the circuit level, but if the controls overloaded, the sensors themselves would be of little value.

Chekov pulled himself up just as Kirk stepped up to the upper bridge level. "Captain, we're just about to test."

The technician closed the access bay and the console came alive. Lights and screens brightened and the hum of the controls added their rhythm to the din of the bridge. It completed a song of sorts, and suddenly the bridge sounded *right*.

One hand touching a set of controls, and the other flipping three switches, Chekov brought the sensors online.

As if summoned at that very moment by his station, the turbolift doors parted and Spock glided toward them. McCoy took a step toward the Vulcan, but didn't scan or otherwise examine him. A certain tension bathed the bridge. Was Spock himself? Certainly not—he was maintaining a meld with Meshu who was five decks below. But would that link change him in the same way his link with Berlis had? Kirk didn't think so—but he wasn't sure, and perhaps some doubt showed on his face. A crew always followed their captain's lead, and he didn't have the luxury of uncertainty.

To augment his confidence in Spock, Kirk gestured to the science station. "Excellent timing as usual, Mister Spock. We need you at sensors."

"Technically, Captain, I should point out that both Meshu and I will be at this station."

"Of course," Kirk said, and hoped his voice remained free of trepidation.

"You are relieved, Ensign."

Chekov nodded and returned to navigation. Kirk looked at Spock for a long moment as the Vulcan turned to the sensors. When the captain returned to the command chair he found McCoy was watching Spock as intently.

"Engaging scanners," Spock said as Kirk lowered himself into the center seat.

Before Kirk could order a tactical screen onto the main viewer, the turbolift doors opened again. Scotty went straight to the engineering station and hovered near DeSalle.

"Main power's restored, sir."

"Scotty, you're taking your timing cues from Spock

now," Kirk told him, but the cheer in his tone felt false and he wondered if it sounded as empty.

"All decks report ready, Captain," Uhura announced.

"Red alert." Kirk thumbed a button on the arm of his chair. "Let's be ready for anything." He nodded at Spock. "Tactical."

The forward screen flashed to life and filled with data. A graphical representation of the *Enterprise* was at the center, then shrank to a dot as the image shifted to include the local part of the Isitri system.

"Damn," McCoy breathed when he saw it, and Kirk felt his jaw drop. Spock clung to his sensor cowl and everyone else stood ready.

"Battle stations!" Kirk called.

They'd taken too long. The Odib were already here, and Berlis's Isitri forces were ready to engage them.

EIGHTEEN

*B*attle stations, battle stations. All hands: battle stations. This is not a drill. Repeat: This is not a drill."

Too long. He'd waited too long. Kirk took the heavy blame and pressed it into his chest. He should have put Spock and Meshu on a shuttle and sent them to Isitra Zero. He should have risked it—a calculated risk. But he hesitated, hoping to see them along himself, to keep an eye on Spock as if he could use his will to snap the Vulcan back into the fold if Berlis grabbed hold. It was a foolish delay.

The Odib filled the outer system, massing most of their numbers in the penumbra of the gas giant, protecting themselves from Colony First and its new weapon.

Just as *Enterprise* poked out of the clouds, the lead Odib ships fired guided charges that swam toward the colony. Only when the sensor weapon was destroyed would they be able to make a clean break for Isitra Zero.

Berlis's fighters couldn't venture forth fast enough to stop the Odib missiles, and didn't even try. As the missiles got closer, the new offensive sensor weapon snapped into the arsenal, quickly disabling them so they fell toward the planet. Hot with friction as they crashed into the atmosphere, they rained down, burning quickly to vapor.

Revealing herself to both sides, *Enterprise* sped forward, placing her massive form between the opposing fleets. No one fired. No ship moved. The imposing Federation starship was three times larger and generally more powerful than any of the vessels gathered around her. Collectively, either fleet could defeat the *Enterprise,* but neither side wanted to begin a battle that would leave itself open to attack.

Kirk sat anxiously forward, and imagined the admirals of each fleet were doing the same on their ships. Or was Berlis directing his fleet from the safe confines of an Isitra Zero bunker? There was no way to be sure.

"Steady as she goes, Sulu," the captain said.

The *Enterprise* couldn't block the Odib and the Isitri from fighting if they wanted to, but her appearance obviously shocked them. Both probably thought her destroyed. They wondered now what she would do next.

So did Kirk. Did he fire on the invading vessels in an attempt to warn them off from their own destruction? Did he engage the Isitri and hope they backed off? The thought of militarily engaging what essentially were innocent people acting against their wills was not what he had bargained for when hoping to make first contact with the Isitri.

He kept his eyes on the main viewscreen, which was now split into two tactical displays showing each fleet. Kirk then turned slightly back toward Uhura. "Raise the Odib. I want to talk to Admiral Das."

"Aye, sir."

"Kirk on communications channel zeta," Sheh said after looking over the comm officer's shoulder. "Flagged urgent."

Das frowned, his brow weaving tightly inward. Three minutes into when the battle was to begin, they were at a standstill. The first salvo was destroyed, but it was to be a distraction for a second volley, in the hopes that the Isitri weapon could not cope with another attack so quickly. Kirk's surprising imposition ruined that tactic.

"Down here," the admiral grunted, gesturing to the screen off the side of his chair. He didn't want his strategic charts removed from the large center screen.

Some sort of Federation flag or standard appeared first. Then Kirk came into view. The bridge of his ship *was* impressive: large and colorful with a flurry of activity. Kirk sat confidently in a center seat similar to Das's but with less equipment attached to it. Perhaps Kirk wasn't a hands-on commander. Das was.

Federationites were an interesting breed, varied in their form. Different colors, at least one had ears shaped different from the rest, and all seemed to have hair on their heads but not their chins, the opposite of the Odib. Das stroked his beard and tried to picture himself with hair on his head, but only fleetingly as he knew he'd look ridiculous.

When he was done sizing Kirk up, he was ready to talk. "This is Das. Speak."

He'd been harsh to see how Kirk would react, and the Federationite didn't blanch or falter. *"This is Kirk. Listen."*

A smile could have appeared on Das's face if he'd let it. He liked people who were direct and unflinching. "I'm listening."

"I'm not confident of the security of this channel so I'll be brief." Kirk stood and looked intently at Das. *"I need you to stand down your fleet. The weapon that destroyed your torpedoes will do the same to your ships. Your shields will be useless."*

Das glanced at Sheh-Keshemger for confirmation. Her shoulders rolled in an uncertain shrug.

"There's no way to know," she said. "Scans of the weapon are difficult to decipher."

"We have a large fleet, Captain," Das told Kirk. "They can't destroy all of us before we raze them."

Obviously frustrated, Kirk's face tightened. *"Admiral—"*

With a raised hand, Das cut him off. "You don't know this situation, Jamesty-Kirk. Your people have no personal stake in our fate, nor do you have the history of death visited on you by the Isitri. If you attempt to stop us, you become our enemy, and will be vanquished along with the troublesome mind's forces."

A nod to Sheh indicated Das wanted the transmission ended. She motioned for the communications officer to do so, but did not leave the admiral's side.

"I know you have doubts," he said before she could speak. He met her eyes and in a low whisper said, "I understand." It was his way of saying he also had reservations, but it would have been inappropriate for him to say so on his own bridge.

Sheh nodded grimly. There was a congress of world leaders who had entrusted him with protecting the homeworld, and that weighed on him. How could he trust Kirk—this man he didn't know, who had some unknown agenda, and was obviously aligned with the Isitri?

He couldn't. His instinct told him Kirk was trustworthy, but for all he knew the *Enterprise* captain was a speaking telepath who was held by the troublesome mind and broadcasting a trusting aura.

No, Kirk could not be trusted. Das would certainly lose a great number of his forces, but the Isitri would be sent back to preindustrial times—and they would never be allowed into space again. Those were the consequences of breaking the treaty, and that is what would be done.

He would attempt to avoid dealing with the Federationites, but should they get in his way, it would be their mistake.

The screen returned to the starscape view and Kirk sighed. He was sympathetic to Das's predicament and respected his determination, but that left the captain with his own dilemma.

"Mister Spock." Kirk nodded and went over to the rail beneath the Vulcan's station.

Spock swiveled his chair toward the captain and calmly waited.

"What are the chances Meshu—with your help—could pull control of the Isitri colonists from Berlis?" Kirk asked.

Spock considered the question quietly. "Unlikely," he said finally.

"Is that your judgment or Meshu's?" McCoy asked.

"Both. The longer Berlis is in control of his people, the more difficult it is to wrench them away from that control. Ending his life would be shocking enough to sever the connection abruptly and they would notice the immediate absence but the colonists have been linked to him for years. It's why he was able to take short visits to Isitra Zero without them noticing his power over them had lapsed. When the loss of the connection is gradual, an individual's will is slow to reassert itself."

"But if Meshu can abruptly lock Berlis out . . ." Kirk said.

"That is not a struggle to be fought in the minds of the inhabitants of Isitra Zero, let alone those of the colonists." Spock spoke so matter-of-factly, as if there were zero doubt about this most uncertain enterprise. "That battle is one we must wage in Berlis's mind with a direct link."

"We?" That hadn't been the plan, Kirk thought, but he also hadn't thought through the exact details. The original idea was that with Spock's mental disciplines taught to her, Meshu would be able to wrench control away from Berlis while also keeping him out of her head. Now, it sounded as if Spock was talking about being the link between Berlis and Meshu himself. "You? Personally?"

"I have been attempting to teach Meshu the protections I employ that block Berlis from my mind," Spock said. "We've found the Isitri brain is incapable of several of the necessary Vulcan mental restraints. If we are to succeed, it will be necessary to initiate a meld between myself and Berlis. While Meshu rips control away from him among the people, I will secure his mind so he cannot wrest them back from her."

Kirk felt a cold sweat break across his neck. "*You'll* be the conduit?"

"I must be."

Was McCoy right all along? He certainly thought so: "You'll open your mind to Berlis," the doctor exclaimed, incredulously. "And just let him in."

"If Meshu is to succeed in pulling the Isitri people to her will, and away from Berlis's, we must work together."

It seemed logical, within the context of what Kirk had been told about the situation, but the source of that information was Spock.

"Pretty damn dangerous, if you ask me, Jim," McCoy said.

Spock tilted his head, a Vulcan type of shrug. "The odds this will succeed make it a reasonable calculated risk."

"Do I want to know the odds?" Kirk asked.

A lifted brow was the captain's only answer. Truth be told, he didn't want to know the odds, not specifically. Because as foolish as it all now sounded . . . it was the only plan available to them. Knowing just how stacked against them things were would only cause worry he didn't have time to deal with.

"We have to get you to Isitra," Kirk said, turning

toward the main viewer. "And simultaneously stop the Odib from destroying the colonists—and their home-world."

"There is no other way," Spock assured him.

So it seemed, but was it true? McCoy had pointed out—correctly—that if all this time Berlis had been connected to Spock, this would be exactly what he'd want the Vulcan to do: bring Meshu and himself to Isitra Zero where they could be joined permanently to the Isitri mind-link.

How sure was Kirk that Spock *was* himself? He was supposed to know if he wasn't, but that was before Spock melded with Meshu. Now Spock was necessarily different. He wasn't just himself, but a Spock-Meshu hybrid.

As the captain studied his first officer's sharp Vulcan features, he tried to decode the minute expressions Spock allowed to flash occasionally in his eyes and across his visage.

"Captain!" Chekov's call spun Kirk around.

On the main viewscreen, the Odib fleet was moving forward and the Isitri ships were holding back. The colony would respond first with their sensor weapon.

He twisted back to Spock who was already analyzing his console's data. "Sensors can be jammed," Kirk said of the colony's offensive artillery. "What about it?"

Spock was skeptical. "The power needed to attempt such an obstruction would be prohibitive."

Kirk wondered aloud: "We've rerouted circuits to protect them . . . how long can we last against that weapon?"

"Three attacks." Spock checked a calculation. "Perhaps four."

"We're going to be the bait, Mister Spock." Kirk pivoted from his first officer to the main screen and the ensuing battle. The captain knew he was more comfortable dealing with the dilemma of Berlis and Meshu. "We'll distract the Isitri and the Odib," he told Spock, "while you and Meshu take a shuttle for Isitra Zero. Can you get through the remainder of the Isitri defenses?"

Spock rose and relinquished his station to Ensign Cordell. "I believe we can," he said to Kirk.

"Good. Get Meshu, and hurry."

As the Vulcan strode to the turbolift, Kirk swiveled around to meet his gaze. "And Mister Spock . . ." He wanted to tell him to be careful or keep his head about him, but instead let a playful grin tug at the corners of his lips. "Try not to destroy *this* shuttle."

Spock nodded accommodatingly. "I shall endeavor not to, Captain."

NINETEEN

Spock's and Meshu's small shuttlecraft arced speed-ily toward Isitra Zero, cutting a line between the gas giant and the colony's moon.

"The shuttle is away, sir," Sulu reported.

"The Odib fleet is closing in on Colony First," Chekov said from the science station. "Isitri fighters from the colony are moving to intercept."

"Put us between them, Sulu," Kirk ordered and glanced only briefly at the navigational coordinates. "Course one-one-three, mark seven."

As *Enterprise* curved up between the two forces, McCoy leaned in and whispered, "You sure about this, Jim? Maybe I should have gone with them."

Maybe. But sparing the doctor at a time like this

merely to babysit his first officer made little operational sense. "I need you here," Kirk told him as he watched the tactical display. "Things are going to get rough."

"Not too rough—sickbay still has beds filled from the last attack." McCoy headed toward the turbolift. "I'll release those I can back to their cabins. We'll make do."

"I hope you don't have to," the captain said back to him.

As McCoy stepped in, he said not quite under his breath, "From your lips to Spock's pointy ears."

Kirk managed to toss an admonishing look at him just as the doors slid closed.

"The Odib are launching another salvo, sir," Cordell reported. "The colony is firing."

Strings of energy, made visible only with the computer enhancement of the main viewer, flowed forward from the Isitri colony and collided with Odib missiles. Bright sparks flashed and dimmed and the artillery broke apart into large chunks of debris. Only one missile detonated, sending the rest into oblivion, long before reaching their intended target.

Another salvo from the colony reached the Odib fleet itself.

"Block it, Sulu!" Kirk ordered, grasping tightly to the arms of the center seat. "Put us in the way."

The sound of something that was a cross between bacon sizzling on a grill and the crackle of a security cell's force field echoed across the bridge. Tendrils of electricity spat through the shields, across the saucer section, and over the ship's console.

"Circuits holding, sir," DeSalle told them all.

Kirk thumped his knee. "Bless you, Scotty."

As *Enterprise* was struck the Odib fired again. This time the missiles met their targets, smacking into Colony First and erupting into a massive explosion that cleaved the moon's atmosphere with dust and molten debris.

Aghast, Kirk's stomach churned. How many people just died because he'd put his ship between the Isitri weapon and Odib forces?

Hawk-like and vengeful, Isitri fighters spread across the Odib line, firing fine, thin tendrils of energy.

"They've retrofitted their ships with the weapon," Chekov said from Spock's sensors. "Weaker but still disruptive."

This was why the Odib so feared the Isitri. In a matter of hours, with the entire mental resources of both planet and colony forced to focus on a single goal, Isitri technology had taken a giant leap forward. Just two days prior they'd had weapons that couldn't seriously challenge the *Enterprise* one on one. Not anymore.

You are concerned, Meshu said.

It was useless to deny the truth, as the conversation Meshu had with Spock was on a telepathic level. *My ship is in danger,* he told her.

You hide your emotions.

Spock made a minor course adjustment and found Meshu's hand was already on the console, making the necessary changes. *To not reveal one's emotions is not the same as hiding them. I merely do not succumb to emotional displays.*

She looked at him and sensed it was more than that, but accepted his word for now. *Why?* she asked.

It is the way of my people.

Why? she asked, and quickly huffed a puff of air as she perceived his irritation. *I am not a child. I am merely curious. Would you rather I investigate your mind for these answers while we are melded?*

Maintain your discipline, Spock told her.

Then answer me. It wasn't a threat on her part, simply an expression of the fact that if he were interested in responding to her questions and unwilling to further open his experiences to her, he would have to convey the information himself.

My forefathers have a history of great violence due to uncontrolled emotions, he explained. *To counter it, we use reason.*

Do you speak of your Vulcan forebears, or of humans? Certain knowledge was inherent in the meld, so Meshu was aware of Spock's dual heritage.

Yes, he answered simply.

Have you no use for any *emotions?* She looked at him as he flew the shuttle on a far course around the Isitri star, hoping to use the solar radiation to mask their approach. With planetary sensors focused on the outer system, it was a sound tactic.

Emotions are not tools of cognition, Spock told her. *They tell you nothing about the nature of reality.*

Her chin quivered. *Perhaps, but cannot emotions tell you something of yourself?*

He didn't look at her, and instead shut down certain power outputs that could be easily scanned by Berlis's people. *I am already familiar with myself,* he said finally.

Meshu made a chirping laugh. *I know you don't believe you're fooling me, Spock. And I doubt you can fool yourself.*

Emotions exist, Spock said. *To not accept that I have them would be illogical.*

Meshu pressed on. *And to embrace them? Would that be so illogical?*

No, he replied. *But not preferable. Where might it end?*

Happiness? She laughed again. *I am reminding you of your mother.*

Yes, he admitted. *You are.*

Meshu frowned. *I have unsettled you. I am sorry.*

I am not unsettled, Spock told her, and didn't doubt it until she doubted it. He did feel more emotional now that he was connected to her—as he had when he was linked to Berlis. The struggle to keep both Berlis blocked and Meshu disciplined left little energy for the ordering of Spock's own feelings.

She huffed a negating breath. *You work so hard to shield your emotions from others—and yourself. But I am here, with you. Our minds touch. And you have not easily shielded your feelings from me.*

Those had been the sentiments he'd just had, but conceptualized in a slightly different way. One of the disadvantages of a telepathic discussion was the speed of it—there was no time to guard one's thoughts and feelings. *Then I owe you an apology,* he said.

You mustn't. Meshu smiled at him. *I understood why Berlis enjoyed communicating with you. Your mind is refreshing.*

As was his. That wasn't something Spock would have normally shared, but it was true, and Meshu was right—he couldn't easily fool her.

You miss him, she said.

Spock's reply was instant, unshielded. *Yes.*

This will be difficult for both of us.

He need not look in her eyes to know what she felt. Her emotions—her longing—washed over him and called to his own. Through Berlis, Spock had experienced the unbridled emotions of billions of people. He always had the same feelings as anyone, but generally wouldn't allow himself to practice them. Connected to Berlis he could leave his own emotions unexpressed but yet know the sensations of all those whose minds he touched. He didn't wish to admit to himself how much he enjoyed it . . . but Meshu's presence in his mind made such deception—and self-delusion—difficult.

She, too, had a longing that was satisfied via telepathy, and Spock forthrightly asked her how difficult it might be to wrench herself away from Isitra once she reconnected with her people.

I sincerely hope, she said, *that it will not be impossible.*

They shared a silent moment, where neither thought anything. But they both felt an incomparable sorrow. The paths of their respective lives had led them to be so close to happiness, and yet demanded they reject bliss in favor of morality.

A choice, Spock told himself and Meshu, *is the root of all morality. Without choice, one can have no moral code.* It was a tenet of Vulcan philosophy, and he recited it to reassure himself—and Meshu—that they had chosen the proper course. *In a vacuum bereft of alternatives, there can be no values. And without values, there can be no reason for a code of ethics.*

She understood, and also didn't fully comprehend why he was explaining such a simplistic thought.

Because, he told her, *what gives our lives meaning is which alternatives we choose. If we have no options, if we can take but one path, we are by definition slaves.*

Their eyes met, and it seemed to make their connection stronger.

We each choose our paths based on the values we as-sign to ourselves, and others. I value the liberty of the Isitri people above my own pleasure.

Meshu made an affirmative gasp. She understood.

You must do more than understand, Spock told her. *You must agree that it is also your goal.*

Their connection being what it was, she would not be able to convince him she was as resolute as he. *I can only promise to try, Spock.*

He silently accepted her frank admission that she was not fully committed to their objective.

And I hope, she added, *that I do not weaken your resolve with my own.*

Spock had considered that possibility before McCoy had even mentioned it. *Indeed.*

Energy plumes from the Isitri fighters raked across *Enterprise,* covering her in electrical flame. *Enterprise* threw javelins of blue energy at its attackers, creating plasma eruptions and jettisoning coolant into space.

"Kirk protects us," Sheh said urgently. "He ob-structs the Isitri forces."

A cascade of explosions rumbled beneath her, shak-ing her stride as she wobbled to Das's command chair.

"Some are getting through," he said.

"They have conventional weapons," Sheh told him and held up a tactical tablet for him to view. "Less than half their fleet have this new sensor weapon."

"Good." Das poked at the screen of her tablet, indicating the ships he wanted targeted first. "We'll repay the favor to Jamesty-Kirk by finishing those he cannot."

"Phasers to disable only, Sulu." Kirk knew that was a good thought, but unlikely to be easily followed. Guesses could be made as to the strength needed to put a ship's engines offline, but who could say what else was damaged in the process? A degree this way or that and a critical system could be vaporized.

Sulu accepted the task nevertheless. "Aye, sir."

"The Odib are engaging the Isitri we can't occupy," came the tense report from the starboard aft. Cordell was young, an ensign like Chekov but with less experience. Kirk would almost prefer the Russian split in two—half of him at Spock's sensors, the other at navigation. In battle, he opted for the man's prowess at tactics and torpedoes.

"Sulu, disable Odib ships as well, if in range." Kirk let out an exasperated breath. "We're not taking sides."

Soon the Odib were firing on *Enterprise* as well. Conventional disruptors, weaker than those of the Klingons or Romulans—but when coming from the dozens of ships that swam around them like so many lightning bugs on a warm summer's night . . .

Despite now engaging the Odib as well, Kirk felt like he was taking a side. This was all to save the Isitri. If he really wanted to stop the Odib from destroying Isitra Zero and the colony, all Kirk needed to do was destroy the capital of Home Zero and the bunker below. *Enterprise* could do so in a matter of minutes. Morally that option was close to him and yet he was causing casualties on both Odib and Isitri fleet ships, calculating—hoping—that in the long run fewer lives would be lost.

Berlis's fighters dove toward *Enterprise,* skimming away from her phasers and layering the ship with tendrils of disruptive energy.

Working in unison, Sulu and Chekov brought their vessel's sharp fangs to bear and raw bars of energy connected with first one Isitri ship, then another, sending both off course in opposite directions.

Another three fighters swooped in, firing the Isitri offensive sensor spread.

"Circuits holding," DeSalle reported. "No significant damage."

Yet, Kirk thought. *Yet.*

As each ship hobbled away the captain made a mental calculation of how many injured there might be . . . and how many dead. The Odib could be said to have chosen their fate, but these Isitri did not. Berlis's destiny was thrust upon them, and they simply believed it to be their own.

"Another Isitri fighter, sir."

Another. How many would he have to fire on?

He wanted to have Uhura contact Spock. He needed

to know how close they were to landing on Isitra Zero. But they couldn't chance a transmission that might give away the shuttle's position. Kirk would have to trust that it was going well—and trust that Spock and Meshu could complete their mission before both the Isitri and Odib fleets were devastated. And before *Enterprise* was as well.

We've been discovered. Unable to sign, his hands busy on the controls, Spock had to let Meshu know telepathically. A high-pitched squeak expressed her shock as the Isitri fighters fired on the shuttle.

They've equipped their vessels with similar sensor weapons to what the colony developed. Spock engaged in evasive maneuvers that would bring him closer to Isitra Zero's atmosphere, but zigging toward it meant having to zag away, and for every two steps forward he had to jump one back.

Shields are useless to us, he told Meshu as he routed power away from those circuits in the hopes they would be reserved for now and could be bypassed later.

Meshu's thin fingers gripped the sides of her chair tightly. *We shall die!* One could not scream telepathically, but the urgency of her thought was evident.

Calm, Spock suggested, and she used his stillness of psyche to compose herself. *Help me,* he asked of her. She began hitting buttons, unsure of what they did, but through Spock knowing exactly their purpose.

A series of shots sizzled across the shuttle's dorsal plates as it veered into the atmosphere. Circuits crackled and failed and when Spock attempted to switch to the unused shield relays, they overloaded, failing instantly. Without shields, the outer skin quickly heated, and a burning trail of smoke streamed behind them as they fell through the stratosphere.

A powered landing was impossible without circuits through which they could route power. And an unpowered landing meant death on impact.

Meshu was oddly calm. She said good-bye to Spock and was thankful she would at least meet her end on her home planet. *Let the soil of Home Zero accept me back.*

TWENTY

The plan, such as it was, had been to distract the Isitri and Odib—keep them from fighting each other by forcing them to engage the *Enterprise*. But there were too many ships in each fleet to sustain that tactic, and Kirk had to dart from skirmish to skirmish, blocking some ships from taking blasts, and surgically removing other ships from battle by disabling their engines. But casualties were going to occur, and the running tally the captain kept in his head weighed on him oppressively. Every slice of phasers added to it.

"Fire."

An Isitri fighter dorsal strut was sheared off, sending the ship off course at an odd angle, plasma flame sputtering behind it.

"Fire."

An Odib engine vent erupted into space, throwing the vessel into a tight spin, away from the Isitri line.

"Fire"

Shields were hit on two more ships, one from each fleet. They each spun around and unleashed their own weapons—not on each other, but on the *Enterprise*. She took the salvos, shuddered through them, and returned the volley.

Pulling punches was not easy for a starship battling two fleets that were trying to destroy each other. One ship had been launching torpedoes into another— destroying both. The shockwave disabled other vessels nearby, and they were going to lose life support. *Enterprise* couldn't beam the people aboard. Lifeboats exploded away from the area, spiraling toward Colony First. With luck they'd survive a crash landing. Those pulled into the gas giant's atmosphere would be crushed.

Kirk's private, morbid tally grew.

The battle waged on. But as Kirk anxiously ordered *Enterprise* to take the brunt of yet another firefight between the two enemies, he knew of no other solution. This was the most moral choice he could make. It was hopefully buying Spock the time he needed.

There was no time to view the ground below in any detail. There were no sensors left to scan for the safest

landing pad. Spock and Meshu relied on her memories
of the capital city—memories of an adolescent girl, who
had been taken from her home many years ago.

The shuttle dropped quickly. Meshu wanted to
reach out to the nearest Isitri. Through that, she'd be
able to understand the changes to the city and could
direct Spock where to glide in.

You mustn't, he warned her. Connecting to any Isitri
mind was the same as tapping Berlis on the shoulder
and alerting him to their plan.

The last of the unburned circuits to which Spock
could switch finally sizzled offline. As the wind howled
through cracks burned into the bulkheads, he escaped
the pilot's chair and pried open an access panel in the
deck.

The shuttle vibrated around them as Spock's fingers
reached for the manual charge release for the emergency landing bags.

Meshu felt the explosion all around her and a high-
pitched bleat screeched through her nostrils.

The shuttle hit the ground and bounced three times.
Spock grabbed for Meshu, and hugged her around her
seat back, pinning them both to the stationary chair. Had
he not, they'd have bounced around the cabin like rag
dolls.

Outside, high-impact balloons were softening the
landing as best they could. What would have been

crushing death was high-g oppression, but they lived.

The rocking back and forth stopped as abruptly as it had begun but Meshu's bleating continued until Spock pressed into her telepathically.

Calm. We are safe. Calm.

Spock pulled her toward the hatch. He grabbed his tricorder, a phaser, and made sure his communicator was still intact.

Still in shock and shaking with fear, Meshu looked out on her home planet for the first time since she was a child. She stumbled out the hatch. She looked around, wobbled weakly forward, and touched a tree . . . then collapsed into it, holding it close to her, and sobbing gently.

Zero, she said over and over to herself. *Zero. Zero. Zero.*

Allowing her a private moment to console herself and regain control, Spock surveyed the area. It was an open glade covered in fern-like plants and short grass with scattered bushes and trees. He assessed the shuttle: crumpled, pitted, scorched, but intact enough. Spock thought of the human saying: Any landing after which one was ambulatory was acceptable.

Tricorder readings told Spock the capital was less than two kilometers away. Under the city was the bunker complex where Berlis and the local council were probably sequestered. Isitri security forces, Spock knew from his previous link with Berlis, would be organized against an Odib infantry landing—not against two stealth infiltrators.

We must go, Spock told Meshu, placing his hand under her elbow—trying to bolster her both physically and mentally.

The city is close, she said.

Spock showed her the tricorder scan of the area. *Access to the underground is closer still. There is an entrance tunnel nearby.*

We must go, she echoed.

They must go, the military advisers pled to Berlis. *Our forces cannot be deployed in such a widespread configuration. We need them at Colony First!* He saw the tactical maps in their minds. He touched the concern in their hearts. He knew they were right, but instinct told him not to push those ships too far into the system, even if Colony First needed reinforcements.

We will lose our link should we move those vessels, Berlis worried to them. *Can we not send support from Zero Home?*

His commanders complained it would take too long. *The* Enterprise *has disabled more than half our fleet, Berlis.*

But Kirk battles the Odib as well, diminishing their numbers, another of the fleet captains offered.

If Berlis allowed the link to be broken, he would

not be connected to his Colony First home, and they were most comfortable to him. Could he leave them in a time of need? A time of fear? Many had already died in the initial Odib strike on their homes. For Berlis to abandon those families now, deserting them . . . *I cannot sanction it. Please, I implore you,* Berlis told the commanders, *do not pull those ships from their locations.*

We shall not, they all agreed. *It would be wrong to abandon the colonists.*

Berlis gasped an affirmative breath. Chista, who sat to his side, did as well. They smiled at each other, nervously reassuring one another and the other members of the capital council as well.

On Colony First, those who had known Berlis the longest bittersweetly rejoiced that he would remain in contact with them, even as they jointly mourned with him over their dead.

When death occurred, every disconnection was a painful slap to their collective psyche. They all wished that the Odib and *Enterprise* would soon see reason and stop their unwarranted attacks on the Isitri.

"This Kirk is the devil!" Das spat that at the screen of tabulated losses that appeared before him. "With one hand he mends our wounds, with the other he reopens them!"

Exposed cables crackled above the Odib admiral,

sputtering electricity and filling the bridge with smoke.

Isitri fighters converged on their vessel, slamming conventional disruptors and torpedoes with their new sensor weapon. Sheh stumbled down to the Das's chair, nearly taking his head off with her arm as she reached out to stabilize herself. He ducked and grabbed for her, pulling her toward him.

"Admiral," she said shakily, "secondary systems are failing. Three decks have lost life support. Explosive decompression has forced emergency bulkheads to engage, trapping thirty crew in those areas."

Frustrated, infuriated, exasperated, Das-Dosiame wished his will had destructive force: Were it so, Kirk's ship, the Isitri fleet, the entire star would wink out of existence.

"We cannot help them," Das growled. "We may not be able to help ourselves."

Another salvo from the Isitri made the deck underneath them, the bulkheads around them, and the bones within them tremble. Debris crashed down from above. Thick slabs of bracing sliced down, cutting into Das's head and pushing themselves through Sheh's stomach. She collapsed across his chair with a weak groan.

The lights flickered, the engines wavered, and hope drained away with the blood that trickled from their wounds.

TWENTY-ONE

There were guards, as Spock assumed there would be. A Vulcan walking in front of them would be a shock that could be used to his advantage—but only once. After that, all other guards would know Spock was on Home Zero. And so would Berlis. For Spock to stay out of sight, Meshu would have to be the one to subdue the sentries.

He handed her his phaser, and concentrated on the way it worked. She gasped her understanding.

It's so small, she said, and Spock explained how much pent-up energy was in the small container. It could, if overloaded, destroy the entire bunker complex.

She protested its use—perhaps she would operate it incorrectly.

You will not. Spock studied her knowledge of Isitri anatomy, however, and gave her a second option.

Leaving Spock in a corridor alcove, Meshu approached the first set of guards. Both women paid her no mind at first, until they realized Meshu was all but invisible: a person was walking up to them, but was only present physically and not mentally. Before they had a chance to react, Meshu stretched out both hands. She pressed in on each guard's neck, executing an Isitri version of the Vulcan neck pinch.

They crumpled into two respective masses of gangly limbs. Meshu was so shocked about her success that she nearly fell over with them.

Spock rushed forward and placed a hand on each guard's temple. Even unconscious, they could relate their last waking thoughts telepathically, and it was better for Spock to pull them into his link with Meshu than it was to leave them free to convey to Berlis that someone was in the bunker.

Taking them carefully from the corridor, Spock placed them both out of the way, in the alcove that had just hidden him.

They will know where Berlis is, Meshu suggested.

Yes.

Before leaving the guards to their sleep, Spock searched their minds. *Where is Berlis?*

The women were confused, disoriented, but they

felt a familiarity with Spock, despite never having melded with him before. *Berlis knows you,* they both told him.

Where is Berlis? Spock asked again.

Without deceit, they thought of his location. Meshu saw it too, and flooded Spock with dread and disappointment. *Protected. We cannot reach him. Too many sentries.*

He eschewed the emotional torrent and tried to calm her. Spock's serene attitude centered her and Meshu attained a more logical mind-set. But they both knew that Meshu's passions were taxing Spock's ability to keep Berlis out and Meshu calm. And now with two more Isitri in the mix, his burden was growing exponentially.

There are at least twenty-seven guards between us and the council room, Meshu said. Spock knew this already and gasped.

He leaned down again, fingertips touching pressure points on the skull of one of the guards.

There is a room, Spock said, *next to the chamber. Unattended. Empty.* He removed his hand and stood up straight again.

You need to touch *Berlis to connect to his mind,* Meshu said.

"No," Spock huffed. *There is an increased danger. Other minds will be present and I may touch their thoughts before finding Berlis. If I do, they will alert him.*

Meshu was nervous and it pricked Spock, peppering him with yet another unwanted feeling. *Compose yourself,* he urged her. *We must go now. The way is clear.*

Meshu frowned anxiously. *But to an empty room.*

"Secondary deflector dish circuits compromised," Scotty called out. "Bypassing to tertiary."

They needed the deflector more than they needed weapons. At the speeds necessary for battle, any fragments of wreckage the mêlée had created—a hull plate or stray shard of rubble—would crash right through the *Enterprise*'s skin if not for the deflector array.

And there was much debris. What vessel remains weren't locked into orbit of Colony First or the nearby gas giant either floated out into space or fell quickly into atmosphere. Three entire ships had begun such a descent toward their doom. *Enterprise* had tractored two of them to safety, even as it battled their comrades. The third had no life signs.

In some ways the battle was easier than Kirk had considered. The Odib had taken out the most powerful Isitri weapon—and while the Isitri fighters had a smaller scale version of the offensive sensor artillery, Scotty's protected circuits and double backup nodes had allowed *Enterprise* to hold its own against over-whelming forces.

The problem was that the ships opposing them were looking to destroy Kirk's vessel, whereas he only hoped to disable theirs. As the battle waged on, the first ships they'd put out of action had made repairs and returned to combat.

"What we need," Kirk said as he directed Sulu to fire on a specific vessel on the tactical display, "is a way to take them all out at the same time."

"Aye," Scott said, "but how?"

Kirk ruminated as the bridge shook around them. They were taking fire from all sides. Two Isitri ships concentrated their sensor fire on one of the engineering decks and suddenly *Enterprise* had a massive power fluctuation.

Scotty grumbled out orders to his people as DeSalle and another crewman worked switches, bypassing more lines.

The lights returned and *Enterprise* fired. Both Isitri ships reeled away as chemical flame spasmed from their engines. How many were just injured on those two ships? How many died? Who had gone to sleep when Berlis first touched their minds and would now wake up without an arm, or a leg, or a family?

Kirk had answered a distress call, saved three people from certain death . . . and this is what he'd wrought.

"Mister Scott," the captain called over to his engineer. "If we can't jam their sensor weapon, can we duplicate it?"

Scotty's eyebrows migrated to the middle of his forehead. "Duplicate it? I've not even studied how they did it."

Stepping toward the rail near Scott's station, Kirk intensely focused on his idea, and the sounds of battle—even the quaking of the ship around him—filtered away. "But you understand the principle."

"Aye, we had to in order to protect ourselves."

Kirk pressed his palms tightly against the red rail. "And we're more protected against this particular weapon—more than the Odib or even the Isitri would be."

"Why would we aim it at ourselves?" DeSalle asked.

"I don't want to aim it at all," Kirk said. Every muscle tightened. "I want to broadcast it."

Saving Isitri was not as Meshu had imagined it. She stood nervously in an anteroom used for storing foodstuffs, as her alien comrade—the first mind she'd touched in decades—pawed at the wall of the council chambers. Beyond it was the central Isitri Council, and Berlis, the troublesome mind who controlled them.

Fingers spread and angled in different configurations as he moved, Spock probed for the proper mental signature. He had to take great care. His link to Meshu was a weakness right now. He was maintaining a barricade for himself, for her, and for the two guards they had encountered. While the sentries did not take much effort to block, as they were still unconscious, Meshu's emotional fits still caused Spock to exert himself unnecessarily, distracting from his ability to juggle all the variables. Now, in an attempt to find Berlis's specific mental signature, if Spock faltered and accidentally allowed Berlis in before Meshu was prepared, they would not only fail to save the Isitri, but also would be enslaved to the troublesome mind's will.

Meshu, for her part, was beginning to panic.

What if someone is hungry and comes to this pantry? she asked him. *What if I do not have the strength to quell the war? At most I influenced a few hundred thousand people—but never billions.*

I am here to assist you, Spock reassured her. *You must control your emotions, Meshu.*

She gasped. She knew he was right and appreciated what he was doing for her planet. The *Enterprise* could have simply solved their problem—and the Odib's—by destroying the capital city and Berlis with it. But at every turn Spock and his people had attempted to save as many lives as possible. She should not doubt him. Or herself.

Cold stone beneath his fingertips, Spock pressed down, feeling his thoughts brush against Berlis's for just a split second. *I have found him*, Spock told Meshu. *Ready yourself. I will establish the meld. You must wrench the people from him, and I will seal him off from them.*

I am ready, Meshu said. And both she and Spock knew it wasn't quite true. Soon, so would Berlis.

TWENTY-TWO

There was much happening. Berlis now realized how different helping to lead a planet was from merely assisting a colony. Today he had to direct both. So many had been lost from the link. Anger trickled up from the families of the dead, but Berlis asked people to understand the fear of the Odib and the Federation. While it was necessary to defend themselves, the Isitri people needed to remember how different they were and how those differences worried other races. Compassion would lead to understanding. Eventually. The Isitri would defend themselves until it did.

Understanding, Berlis explained to them all, *comes at the most unexpected moments.* His life had been testament to that.

It is true, Chista expressed. *I did not understand Berlis until I learned more about him, and discovered there was nothing to fear.*

Several others on the council chimed in that their experience had been similar: Bannatyan and Sektu, Kenachin and Gralow. Everyone felt the same. Everyone thought the same.

Information from the captains in the fleet told them that *Enterprise* was beginning to take damage and the tide of battle was perhaps ready to turn in the Isitri favor. There was no joy in learning that the Federation people would have to be ended—especially Spock, with whom Berlis felt he'd begun a robust friendship.

Spock. Just the thought of him made Berlis feel the link might be open and— *Spock?* Was he there? Were his thoughts available? Berlis had felt a flutter of familiarity and thought perhaps the Vulcan had reconnected, if only for a moment.

If *Enterprise* were dying, if Spock were unfortunately injured, perhaps his mind was seeking refuge and he'd seen the error of his ways. Berlis reached out for an instant update on the Federation ship's condition.

Oddly, eerily, only silence replied.

Berlis reached out again. He asked Chista and the others to do the same.

Perhaps one of the connecting ships has traveled out of range, Bannatyan suggested.

Huffing his skepticism, Berlis reached out again—and this time felt a new Isitri he'd never known.

Are you newly conceived, little one? he asked.

No, came the reply. *I am Meshu. I have returned home.*

Returned? Berlis's feelings gushed across the planet: first confusion, then cautious joy, and then fear . . .

Who are you? Berlis asked. *Who is she, Chista?*

Chista hesitated and a coldness suddenly flowed from him. He was unsure of himself, of Berlis, and yet . . . not of Meshu.

I . . . I believe it is working, Spock. Meshu kept her eyes tightly closed. She pushed her mind out—farther than ever before.

Berlis has sensed me, Spock told her. *You must work quickly. He must not be in control when I reveal myself.*

I . . . try. Meshu was under enormous strain. Spock was as well. He was drained, sapped, but they continued coordinating: where Meshu pushed herself to take charge of minds from Berlis, Spock raised barriers to Berlis's touching those minds again.

Fingers pressing deeper into the stone wall, Spock exhausted himself to raise the protection Meshu needed to do her work.

Can you reach the fleet commanders? he asked her.

I feel them, Meshu said. *I cannot control them. I am*

suggesting—but they are not yet listening to my will. All the time she'd been on Zero Home she'd tried to limit her influence over the minds around her. Her life in exile was testament to her inability to do so. Now she was asked to reverse her learned morality and instead not only give in to her nature, but also surpass it.

Difficult at first, it was becoming somewhat easier for her. And with each mind she touched—more pleasurable.

Spock considered warning her against giving into the gratification, but right now he needed her to use it. And . . . he felt the gratification as well and part of him wanted to also give in. So many minds connected to his, so much intellect—it was quite enthralling. Yes, an emotion. He allowed himself to feel, justifying it by reminding himself he needed to use his energy to help Meshu and so must let his emotional guards down.

She needed as much bolstering as he could manage and if he should be unable to pull himself away from Berlis, he would need her to save him from his own trap.

Static crackled across the main viewscreen as Odib attackers punched raw energy across the saucer. "Divert phaser power to shields," Kirk ordered. He hung near the comm on the command chair, waiting for word from Scotty.

The turbolift doors opened and Kirk twisted toward

them, but it wasn't Scott who burst onto the bridge; it was McCoy.

"Bones?"

"Don't you *Bones* me, Captain."

If McCoy called him *captain* in that tone, it meant the doctor had something far up his craw.

The quake of weapons fire staggered McCoy's gait as he stomped toward the command chair.

"I'm busy, Doctor," Kirk snapped, lacking both the time and patience.

"Scotty tells me he's rigging a charge that will likely fry most of the good circuits we have left."

Another tremor forced McCoy to grip onto the arm of Kirk's chair.

Kirk didn't meet the doctor's eyes. He kept his attention on tactical. "Come about, Sulu. Chekov, target to starboard."

"Circuits like life support," McCoy continued as if Kirk had merely paused to pour the doctor a cup of coffee.

"Life support is the most protected," Kirk countered. "As are sickbay systems."

"Are you trying to commit suicide? For all of us?" McCoy sputtered.

Kirk turned to him fully. "Calm down, Doctor. I'm not just ordering my engineer to blow out random systems! We're overloading key nodes that will send out a wave of energy on the same frequency as the Isitri sensor weapon. Yes—it'll fuse a lot of our systems! But we'll knock out all of theirs. Every vessel trying to destroy their neighbor—and us—will be disabled in one fell swoop and without more loss of life."

"Except maybe ours?"

"Yes," Kirk conceded more calmly, even a little tiredly, "it's risky. But we have to buy Spock enough time. And we can't do it firing on every ship in two warring fleets—and getting fired on by them." The captain met McCoy's cool blue eyes. "I can't let two planets destroy each other because of my mistake."

McCoy softened his tone. "You saved a man's life, Jim. You're not to blame for what came from that."

"The road to hell, Doctor." Kirk rolled his jaw and turned away, casting his eyes back on the main viewer. "I paved the road."

"Mister Scott, sir," Uhura said, her voice layered with support and anxiety.

Kirk took another lingering look at McCoy, then thumbed the comm. "Scotty."

"We're ready, Captain. Whenever you give the word."

McCoy stood his ground at the command chair. He nodded encouragingly when the captain glanced at him. He'd come to chastise Kirk and now he stayed to support him.

On the main viewscreen, two Odib ships clashed with three smaller Isitri vessels. Another two rolled toward *Enterprise,* spewing disruptor fire.

Hands pressed tightly on the arms of his seat, Kirk steeled himself and watched the main viewer. "Now, Mister Scott."

Dozens of sensors usually used for passively scanning the universe around them, or actively touching a particular object, flashed alive. A bubble of hard energy spread out from *Enterprise.* The wave pushed into the vessels around them, crackling through the shields and into their control circuits.

A reflection of the force rebounded toward *Enterprise,* the energy bouncing off the multiple contacts. Kirk's ship was buffeted. Circuits exploded, smoke filled the bridge and fans clicked on. Above him, a panel burst open and spewed char and insulation across his neck. McCoy ducked and fell back as the deck shook.

Burning embers rained onto them as the vessel quaked and then went dark.

Sheh blinked in the relative darkness. Only sparks from exposed circuits provided dim crackles of light. She focused on her sense of hearing: coughing, sizzling, creaking, wheezing. She groped toward the command center and called out to Das-Dosiame. "Admiral?"

Tripping over a chunk of debris that had fallen to the deck she collapsed across the command chair with a dull thud and felt Das under her. Her vision adjusted to the dim light and she saw him, eyes open and glazed over, blood draining down his face and into his beard from a slice of metal pressed into his forehead. "Das!" She staggered up and shook him at the same time, trying to rouse him. He slumped. Dead.

Sheh rubbed from her eyes both smoke and tears. She embraced him, something she had dared not attempt when he lived, and choked on her grief. She hoped no one heard her soft sobs over the din of their own misery.

With a gulp, she held down her anguish and bolstered her determination. Das's will would be carried out. He was the admiral, and Sheh would take the ship and follow his last orders.

"Admiral Das is dead," she told the bridge. "I am assuming command." Not wishing to remove her commander from his chair, Sheh-Keshemger stepped to the side, but called out her orders. "I need a full status report," she told whomever could manage. "See to the wounded, see to the vessel, and try to raise the fleet." If the ship was a total loss, she'd transfer the command standard to another vessel and continue the battle from there.

Both Das and Sa would be avenged.

"Emergency lights." Kirk reached down and pulled McCoy to his feet as the lights flickered on. Smoke was already clearing. Certain circuits protected themselves by shutting down when in danger of overloading—

bridge lights and fans included. Sometimes circuits were saved in that manner, and sometimes not. This time they survived.

McCoy nodded his appreciation as he regained his footing. Behind him, Kirk zeroed in on DeSalle who manned the engineering station in Scotty's absence. "Damage report."

Coughing out an answer, DeSalle choked on the smoke that settled from above. "Status coming in now, Captain." He waved away the fumes and punched at his console. "Life support coming back online," he said. "Deflectors down, sensors down, thrusters barely at station-keeping." He turned to Kirk and nodded, encouraged. "All decks report power being restored."

"Mister Sulu."

"Helm is responsive, but without sensors . . ."

"Understood." Kirk punched his arm chair comm. "Kirk to engineering."

"Scott here."

"I need sensors, Scotty."

"Aye. We're workin' on it, sir." The engineer's Scottish burr couldn't conceal an unspoken frustration. *"We're rerouting backup circuits to those that're not, but we can't withstand more attacks from the Isitri weapon."*

"How long before we're maneuverable?"

The engineer made a soft sigh. *"Six minutes, sir."*

"Good work, Scotty. Kirk out." Thumbing the

comm back off, the captain exchanged a grim glance with McCoy. They both knew that only one of Berlis's ships needed to have survived the sensor blast to disable *Enterprise* for good. That vessel could be moving toward them now, ready to pounce, and there was nothing they could do about it. They wouldn't even know until it was too late.

"What now?" McCoy asked.

"We wait," Kirk said, pressing his lips into a thin line. "And hope Meshu and Spock can succeed."

McCoy didn't ask what would happen if that didn't occur. He just crossed his arms and groaned.

TWENTY-THREE

There was a balance to what Spock was attempting. He walked a mental precipice tenuously. As Meshu reached out for more Isitri minds, Spock blocked those thoughts from Berlis. The troublesome mind didn't notice, just as one might not notice a room gradually cooling off or growing dimmer. But there would be a point when Berlis would suddenly become aware that his sphere of contact was smaller than it should be, and not just because of the deaths. Meshu had distracted Berlis by introducing herself, but she'd learned the disciplines Spock had taught her, and Berlis neither controlled her, nor saw the deception.

Having known Berlis as well as he did, Spock knew

trickery would not have been easily discerned. His naïveté was genuine. He'd lived in a society where false-
hoods were uncommon and once he imposed his will
on those around him, what lies were there to tell?

With his own emotional defenses down, Spock was
sad. Hurting Berlis, as he knew would happen, was
anathema to the Vulcan.

Meshu's anxiety didn't help matters. *It is time,* she
told Spock. *We have enough.*

No, we must continue. The fewer minds touching
Berlis's, the easier it would be for Spock to do what
he must, he told her. And while that was true, he
wondered if he had an ulterior motive. He understood
Meshu's pull toward the link of Home Zero. He craved
it. And, like her, he would miss it when it was gone.

Part of him wondered what he might do if Meshu
was unable to fulfill her part of the plan, and how he
might handle being trapped with Berlis. Was he considering that contingency because he secretly wished
it? McCoy would suggest so. The doctor was often
entirely off about his supposed insights into Spock's
psyche . . . and yet other times he was spot on. Most
recently he was between those two extremes: It wasn't
Berlis who controlled Meshu or Spock—it was their
own passions. Meshu didn't want to give up the link,
and neither did Spock.

Overwhelmed with fear that when the time came she
would be unable to muster the will to leave it behind,

Meshu wanted to get the event over with. Conversely, Spock wanted to delay until he was certain he had control of his desires, and not the reverse.

Meshu insisted now was the time. Spock's feeling was that he wasn't quite ready, even if she was.

Feeling. His *feeling*. That was his mistake, he chided himself. Feelings did not explain reality. They were not, as he told Meshu, tools of cognition. One's emotions could not be factored in. Couldn't be. Shouldn't be.

Wouldn't be.

Yes, Spock told her. *Now is the time. Prepare yourself.*

Berlis was fascinated by Meshu. *Where did you come from? Why have I never known you before? Tell me about yourself.* His questions were innocent, so he didn't understand why Meshu was being coy and would not open her mind with the answers.

I was born in Dalinga Bektab, Meshu told him. It wasn't an answer to any of his questions and Chista bristled on Berlis's behalf.

I know no one named Meshu from Bektab province, the council man said. *Why are you bashful with us? We represent the capital council.*

You do not know me? Meshu asked. *I know you.*

I promise I do not know you, or do not remember you, Berlis said. *Chista, search your mind.*

For an inexorably long time, Chista did not answer.

Berlis looked at him across the council room and rapped on the table twice to get his attention. Chista frowned at Berlis.

Chista, what is wrong? Berlis asked.

Chista only frowned.

Chista? What troubles you?

Berlis blinked several times in succession. Something was terribly wrong. Chista sat living, breathing in and out, but was dead in his mind, as if he'd had a sudden, massive stroke or—

No, something else had happened.

Bannatyan? Berlis searched for another mind he knew well. There was no reply. *Bithnush? Golo?* They were all from his clan—their minds more in tune with his than anyone else's. *Where were they?*

Even a sudden plague would not rip people from the link like this.

Panic coursing through his veins, Berlis rose and shook the person next to him. He blinked into their eyes, and their only response was to frown at him.

Person after person, male or female, it did not matter. No one spoke to Berlis. All minds were closed to him.

Was he sick? He was sick! He must be!

He ran into the hall and grabbed the nearest sentinel. *Speak to me,* he demanded. *SPEAK TO ME!*

A high-pitched whine escaped his flaring nostrils and he collapsed between the two guards who looked down at him with confusion.

Anyone, Berlis called out, pleading. *Am I dead? Is this death?* Pulling in his legs and placing his head under his left arm, Berlis curled himself into a ball and sobbed.

You are not dead, Spock told him.

SPOCK! You have returned! Berlis's excitement—his total relief—flowed over the Vulcan and he quivered under the emotional torrent.

Yes, I am here, Berlis.

With the flood of emotions—confusion, enthusiasm, fear—came a deluge of desperate questions: *What is happening? Can you help me? Are you well? Am I ill? Help me reason this out!*

An undercurrent of worry peppered Berlis's thoughts: Without his leadership, would the Odib now defeat the Isitri and lay waste to Home Zero?

Epic sadness pressed into Spock's heart, and the disciplines he used to sustain the barriers between Berlis and the planet so that Meshu could take control were going to waver if something was not done to calm the troublesome mind.

Spock decided to explain matters to Berlis, quelling his fear for the planet, first. *Home Zero will be safe because of this.*

Confusion became the strongest emotion—not relief. *What is "this"?* Berlis asked. *What is happening to me?*

Spock felt himself physically tremble, his stomach

twisted in knots. He took his hands off the wall and walked shakily out into the hallway. Around the corner, Berlis was still on the floor, still coiled in on himself. Kneeling down, Spock placed one hand across Berlis's head and the Isitri man's eyes shot open.

In that moment, Spock broke his links to the two guards he'd touched, as well as the minds of the council members he'd blocked from Berlis and handed to Meshu. Spock touched Meshu's mind, peripherally, as he would need help extracting himself, but now his total focus was on wrapping his mental shields around Berlis's damaged psyche.

This is purposeful, Berlis said, aghast. *You are jailing me!*

Yes, Spock said with false dispassion.

The horror violently crashed into Spock, the sentiment palpable.

What have I done to deserve this? Spock, are you not my friend? He was crying now, rocking back and forth under the pressure of Spock's fingers.

My people need me, Berlis screeched in Spock's mind. *I need them!*

The realization of shocking loneliness was washing over Berlis now, and over Spock as well. The Isitri man's mind reached out in every direction, groping for another presence besides Spock. Berlis pressed against the barriers the Vulcan had built around him. Like a coffin, they confined him, buried him, hid him from the universe, and kept the universe from him.

No, he huffed as well as cried to Spock through the meld. *No. NO! NOOOOOO!* A child locked out of his home, Berlis was overwhelmed with fear and panic and a heavy bottomless dread.

Spock collapsed next to him and drew him close. He felt a tear drop to his cheek and flow downward. But still he did not allow Berlis to touch the world he was used to. He denied him access to his home.

I cannot be alone, Berlis wailed. *Please, please, please, I cannot be alone!*

Unable to tear himself away—unwilling to destroy Berlis further—Spock held the frail troublesome mind tightly. *I will stay with you,* Spock sobbed as he replied and severed his last link with Meshu, rejecting the outside world for both of them. *I will not leave you completely alone.*

The turbolift doors opened and Scotty strode to his station. "Sensors restored, Captain," he said and nodded to DeSalle to check the systems monitor. "I've got full impulse available, or warp, but not both. They're sharin' the same control circuits."

Kirk smiled briefly and gave the engineer an appreciative nod. "Thank you, Mister Scott." He crooked a thumb toward Spock's science station. "Chekov, short-range scan, please."

Sliding out from behind navigation, Chekov peered into the scanner; the ensign flipped two switches and put the starscape on the main viewer.

A graveyard of debris—and intact ships—drifted around them. Whatever course a vessel was on when it lost power to its engines was the path it continued on. Kirk hoped none had fallen into the lunar colony's atmosphere or that of the gas giant.

"Life signs?" he asked, his eyes shifting from one intact ship to another on the viewscreen.

"Yes, sir," Chekov said, still examining the blue sensor glow. "All intact vessels have life support." The ensign chuckled in disbelief. "Thirteen Isitri fighters are maneuvering, Captain." He looked up, a proud smile thinning his lips. "They're returning to Isitra Zero."

Leaving the battle theater. Spock and Meshu had gotten through. Kirk breathed a quiet sigh of relief and swiveled around to Uhura, but Chekov grabbed his attention with an urgent call.

"Sir!"

Turning first toward the science station and then looking at the main screen, Kirk saw: a single Odib vessel fired on the retreating Isitri ships. One blossomed into plasma flame and fell quickly toward the gas giant.

"Uhura, raise the Odib. I need to talk with Admiral Das."

• • •

"Admiral Das is dead," Sheh-Keshemger spat bitterly. "No thanks to you, Jamesty-Kirk."

"Stop firing on the Isitri vessels," Kirk demanded. *"They're unarmed and retreating."*

"Did they refrain from firing on our disabled ships?" Burning with anger, Sheh stood tensely, pointing at the command chair and Das's slain body, which she still refused to move. *"His* blood is caked in my beard because you've defended these attackers—"

"You're in their *system,"* Kirk snapped. *"They retreat while you look to raise the death toll out of anger and revenge?"*

"Yes," she snarled. "I am following my admiral's orders to resolve the Isitri threat." A sneer contorted her face. "Once, and forever."

If nothing else, Kirk had at least distracted the Odib with debate. *Keep her talking,* he thought, *and let the Isitri ships get closer to home.*

"Captain," Kirk began.

"Commander," she corrected. *"Sheh-Keshemger."*

"Commander Keshemger." Kirk rose and bowed his head respectfully. "I understand your anger," he said smoothly. "The Isitri began wars that killed millions of innocents."

"Yes."

"And no matter the reason," Kirk continued, "your people have died."

"Yes," she fumed.

He stoked her anger rather than satiated it. "How many blameless Odib died at Isitri hands, just because a troublesome mind like Berlis coerced them to fight you?"

"Millions!"

"Right!" Kirk pointed at her. "So why shouldn't you kill those enslaved Isitri, even if they've now regained their own wills and are returning to their peaceful lives?"

Sheh-Keshemger faltered, began to sputter. *"I—"* Her eyes flicked to the others on her bridge, and stopped on Das. *"He wanted this,"* she said, still angry but her voice softer than before. *"His orders . . ."*

"Were to protect the lives of the innocent," Kirk said. "As any good admiral would ask." The captain shook his head sadly. "Commander, don't act against his morals by following an order given before circumstances changed."

"But next time," she began, the sentence trailing off and her gaze lost in a memory.

Kirk opened his arms as if to reach out to her. "Next time, the Federation will mediate. We'll help to avoid the death of even one Odib or Isitri." He stepped closer to the viewer, closing the virtual distance between them.

"The war is over. Let's bury our dead . . . not add more."

Sheh turned away. *"Yes,"* she said barely above a whisper and motioned to someone offscreen. Two men stepped in and, with care and respect, gingerly removed Admiral Das from his command chair.

Meshu found Spock and Berlis where the sentinels said they'd be, where they were left at her request.

Her Vulcan mentor sat against the gray wall, eyes unfocused, shoulders slumped, hugging her predecessor. Berlis was curled into a fetal position, sobbing softly and rocking slowly.

There was no remnant of Spock in Meshu's mind so she waved a hand before his face, but his eyes did not move.

She searched Spock and found his communicator, and though she could not speak into it, she opened the device and pressed buttons. Lights flashed, though she wasn't sure what they meant and couldn't know if someone said anything on the other end.

Unsure of what to do, she simply told all Isitri to help their neighbors, heal the wounded, and mourn the departed. She knew Kirk would eventually come. *He must. The fleeing fighters see his ship intact,* she thought. If not, she would be stranded, forced to become the one thing she'd always promised herself—and her mother—she wouldn't.

She lowered herself to the floor and sat next to Spock and Berlis. They were the two people on the planet with whom she couldn't connect mentally, so she hugged them both and sadly savored her last hours of bliss before she returned to her solitary life.

TWENTY-FOUR

As *Enterprise* sped from the Isitri system, Meshu felt the link with her people wane. When it finally seemed as if the connection had been severed, she wished them good-bye. Unexpectedly she heard the echoes of billions crying out for her as she slipped away. If someone had shaved off her skin slowly it would have felt less painful. She knew she *could* have remained with them. How could Kirk have stopped her if she really insisted on it? Spock was the only one who could keep her from staying with her people and he was in no state to do so. The thought had crossed her mind a dozen times. She daydreamed about it, planned it, and twice began to tell Kirk that it was her wish. She debated it with herself endlessly until the moment the transporter beam whisked her away.

When Kirk returned to Home Zero, Meshu used the council's interpreter to explain what had happened to Spock and Berlis. Here on *Enterprise* she was without the ability to communicate; the wrist device Spock told her Berlis used was new technology limited to the Isitri ships, and none could be found for her trip home. She thought the captain understood some of her gestures, but he'd been totally inadequate at using them himself. McCoy tried very hard to understand and apparently knew Earth sign language, but it was too different, and was gibberish to her.

Body language, however, was far clearer. Kirk's and McCoy's concern as Spock lay catatonic in their sickbay was obvious. Next to him, Berlis flinched under the restraints that seemed more to keep him from rolling off the bed than anything else.

Meshu knew Berlis's pain and understood that Spock, locked in a meld with him, must understand it as well. Just why he sealed himself in with Berlis was a mystery, but Meshu could guess. As damaged a soul as Berlis was now, Spock had always been. She'd known it when they melded, but assumed the mind in pain they shared was mostly hers. While she had her own burdens, Spock's were heavier. She was exiled from one world. He was self-exiled from two.

If she could talk to him now, perhaps she might be able to help him. Then again, perhaps no one could.

He needed to travel alone on his journey, yet he obviously could not bring himself to do so. Nor could he travel it with help. Instead, he did what Berlis did: collapsed in on himself.

Though Meshu felt more alone than Spock probably ever had, she was still more cheerless for him—and for Berlis—than for herself. She would return to her exile and embrace her adopted family again, but even together, the two men were alone.

Kirk may or may not have asked her village if they still truly loved Meshu and indeed wanted her back; she didn't know. If she had the ability to ask him, she would not want Kirk to tell her. While she had imagined this last visit to Home Zero would cause a hole in her heart, instead she discovered that her new home was, in most respects, filling enough.

True, she would still long for her world, when she slept or when the silence of voices in her mind became too much to endure. But what a small price to pay to know that her first home was safe. That calmed her greatly, and surprisingly she was also comforted by the knowledge that she'd found a new, unexpected yearning for her small village and the faces of her adopted planet.

Many revolutions ago her mother told her that there were some dreams one could attain, and others one could not. Her mother's advice had been for her daughter to attain her dreams by altering them to meet the possible. Meshu had learned to draft her dreams to those things within her reach, and merely think fondly of those she could not. The unattainable goals? She would not waste her energy on them. It would be illogical to do so, she'd discovered—and she could thank Spock for the added insight.

Wishing again that she could reach the Vulcan one last time, Meshu closed her eyes and stretched out her mind to him. To her sorrow, her senses told her there were no telepaths near. Locked in their own exiles, Spock and Berlis were as good as dead to her.

And yet, she sat in sickbay, watching them and still trying to touch their thoughts. Uncertain of how long she had been trying, she was startled when Kirk touched her shoulder and indicated she should follow him.

He spoke as they rode on the turbolift, though the movement of his lips meant little to her and the few signs he attempted were relatively useless—unless he indeed hated her ugly, fat cow.

She couldn't help but smile a little, and what he actually tried to say must not have been funny because he looked at her quizzically a moment, before smiling himself and bowing his head in what may have been an apology.

She remembered the early difficulty of communicating with the villagers who found her. They, too, seemed to assume that if they simply moved their lips carefully or slowly she would somehow divine their meaning.

After many years she could perhaps understand a word or two by lip reading, but to attempt to follow a conversation with that method would surely drive her mad.

As Kirk continued to blather at her, she gasped a lot, affirming whatever he talked about as if she understood, and he took her to their teleportation room and guided her to the brightly lit platform.

He stood fully facing her and the sad and yet somehow charming expression on his face gave her a very warm feeling. What a superior group of people these were, and what an extraordinary leader they had in Kirk. She should like to see them all again someday, under hopefully different circumstances. That was, of course, only if Spock survived. She'd touched him the most, and would not want to entertain the thought that his unique mind was not in existence.

With another bow, which might have been a goodbye, an apology, or both, Kirk signed "thank you" correctly, and curled his short neck to the man in red behind the console.

Light tickled her from within and without, and sparkles enveloped her even though she shut her eyes tightly. When this all faded, she was home.

"Well, Bones?" Kirk had hoped his few minutes away from sickbay would mean he'd be happily surprised upon his return to find that the doctor had come up with a way to sever Spock from Berlis.

McCoy hovered over Spock, watching his vitals, injecting him with different potions. "I still think she was our best bet," he said, waving the hypospray to indicate Meshu.

"I asked her if she could, and she said no."

"What, up here?" McCoy scoffed.

"On Isitra Zero, with the interpreter." Kirk sighed and paced the small sickbay ward. "You'd beamed up with them already. She said . . ." He hesitated. He didn't want to believe it. He couldn't believe it. "She said Spock locked himself in the meld, deliberately."

McCoy turned slowly toward Kirk, grabbing the hand scanner in a tight grasp as if it were ready to fall. "Berlis didn't force him—"

The captain shook his head and whispered, "No."

"Then why?"

Kirk shrugged and he pushed out a long breath. He shuffled over to Spock's bed and thought any moment the Vulcan might snap out of it, stand up, and explain how some inexplicable Vulcan ruse was to blame.

That didn't happen.

"I need him, Bones," Kirk said, and his eyes shifted to Berlis. With the Isitri man's mind completely locked away, he was finally able to have an uninfluenced feeling about Berlis. Right now, that feeling was anger. An unspeakable notion struck Kirk: What if Berlis died? Would Spock be free, or would the shock kill his friend?

Was this why Berlis's nature was to influence those around him? Was it a defense mechanism? Eons ago, did the bird-like creatures that perhaps gave rise to the Isitri defend themselves from predators by broadcasting a nonthreatening aura? If Berlis had no telepathy, would Kirk have turned him over to his own people soon after saving him?

No, he decided. He wouldn't have. His feelings were one thing—his morals another.

"Feelings," Kirk murmured and turned back to Spock. "Bones, Meshu said Spock was crying when she found him. He was *crying.*"

"Well, that's not unexpected," McCoy said. "He was going through an incredible strain."

Finger jabbing at Berlis, the words snapped off Kirk's tongue. "He's not himself. Even now, even if we're not at all influenced by Berlis, Spock is."

"That may be, but where does it get us?" Frustration arched McCoy's brow and heightened his voice. "Everything I've tried—every stimulant, every brain blocker—nothing works! Right now the only sure bet I know is stopping all his brain function. That's called death and I won't cure my patient posthumously." He looked down at Spock a long time, then back up at Kirk, a warmer glint in his eye. "Though lord knows those Vulcan brainwaves can probably survive even death."

"Spock isn't the key." The captain turned to Berlis.

As if reacting to a fever, the frail Isitri man continued to moan and flinch against the restraints. "*He* is."

"I'm not going to kill him, either," McCoy said tiredly as he prepared a nutritional hypo.

"I'm not asking you to," Kirk snapped. The doctor's accusation hit a little too close to home. Would the captain be willing to sacrifice Berlis's life for Spock's? It wasn't even a question. He paced back to the counter opposite their beds and leaned down, laying his palms flat. "There has to be some way to . . ." He searched for the right term for a very wrong notion. "To stop his brain from functioning."

"Yeah," the doctor bristled, "it's called death."

Kirk pounded the counter with a tight fist and bolted upright, burning McCoy with a glare. "Damn it, Bones, we're talking about Spock!"

Facing off against his captain, the doctor straightened as well, tossing the hypospray on the table next to Spock's bed. "I don't care if we're talking about murdering Colonel Green to save Zefram Cochrane! I'm a doctor, not an executioner!" He pointed at his patients almost accusingly. "It's a mind-meld—you kill Berlis and who knows what kind of trauma Spock will suffer."

"I'm asking your medical opinion, Doctor!" Kirk barked. "Is there a way to reduce Berlis's brain function to a bare minimum? Just enough to keep him alive?"

The doctor chewed angrily on the question, then said, "I've not studied this man's physiology enough to know."

"Then study it!" Kirk demanded.

"Fine. See you in ten years." McCoy turned toward the door when he saw Chapel ready to enter. He shooed her off and she retreated.

Arms crossed, Kirk leaned heavily against the bulkhead, cupping his chin with one hand. "We have life-support machines that will keep someone alive when they're in a coma, until—"

"He's not *in* a coma . . ." McCoy's brow wrinkled, an idea changing his expression. "Maybe that's it," he said. "A medically induced coma." He sped into the outer examining room and leaned down to access his desk computer and Kirk followed. "They used to do this sort of thing centuries ago, with sedation," McCoy said, sorting through computer tapes before finding the one he wanted and sliding it into the loader. "About sixty or seventy years ago there was a similar procedure done with localized stasis fields, far more aggressive. It's been rarely used since the invention of cortical suppressors and stimulators . . . but it might limit enough of Berlis's brain function for the mind-meld to be useless." The doctor looked up at Kirk, an embryo of a smile turning his lips. "You can't link an active mind with an inactive one."

"How soon can you be ready?"

"Jim, there are risks." McCoy relaxed his posture and his tone softened. "Berlis might not recover, or Spock could stay linked anyway and—"

So it would be risky, Kirk thought, *and maybe just a false hope, but what other choice is left?* "Do it. Unless you have another way to even attempt to break the meld, short of killing Berlis . . ." He shook his head grimly and sighed. "Just do it. Any assumed risk is *my* responsibility."

McCoy studied the captain's face a few moments, trying to understand whatever it was his psychologist-side wanted to know. Apparently dissatisfied, he frowned, nodded, and got to work.

Gathering the equipment took some time and involved Scotty, two engineering techs, and three medical techs. Kirk watched, and the flurry of activity around Spock and Berlis only reinforced their relative stillness.

Spock had been on the precipice of death more than once. It was the inherent risk of being in space and exploring the unknown. But Meshu said he'd chosen this—that he'd said good-bye to her and told her he was making the right decision for Berlis and himself. That meant his actions weren't necessary to resolve the situation, but were his—and/or Berlis's—desire. As much as the idea of losing his friend worried him, the thought that Spock desired to be cut off from the universe frightened Kirk more.

• • •

"Go ahead, Nurse," McCoy ordered, and Chapel hit the switch on the computer console that had been set up next to Berlis's bio-bed. A hazy light fluttered around the troublesome mind's head from two probes that had been extended above each temple. The glow gave his milky skin and peach fuzz an even paler quality. In the most disconcerting way possible, he looked instantly dead.

The doctor ran his scanner and monitored the screen above the bed. Slowly, the indicator for brain activity slid lower and lower down the scale. Other vital signs decreased as well, and concern pinched McCoy's brows together. He administered the prepared hypo that Chapel put in his palm as soon as he held out his hand, and the levels increased—including the one for mental activity. A battle began to find the level where brain output would be low enough and yet heart and respiration would be high enough. And it took close to an hour before the doctor turned to Kirk and mopped his brow with his shirtsleeve.

Kirk suddenly realized he, too, had been perspiring, and he wiped his hand across his forehead and absently brushed the dew on his pant leg.

"His mind is incredibly strong," McCoy said wearily. "We'd dampen the neural activity, and it's like his brain would catch a second wind, then a third, and a fourth."

As the nurse tended Berlis's now inert form, McCoy and the captain gathered around Spock's bed.

Indicators for the Vulcan's brain activity had also wavered—Kirk and McCoy had both kept an eagle's eye on them. Once Berlis was completely under—as low as he could be placed—Spock's brainwave pattern stabilized.

Pulling another already prepared hypospray from the bedside table, McCoy shared a last, worried glance with Kirk before injecting the Vulcan's arm.

Moments after the hypo hissed its potion into his green veins, Spock's eyes fluttered open. With incredible speed his hand reached out and grabbed McCoy's wrist, wrenching it upward.

He pulled McCoy close until their faces nearly touched and yelled, "Murderer!"

TWENTY-FIVE

W hy did you do it?" Spock demanded, rage and
agony arching his swept brows.

"He's not dead," Kirk shouted, and with some difficulty yanked the Vulcan's hand away from McCoy's
wrist.

The doctor shrank away and Spock's furious eyes
leveled themselves at Kirk. The Vulcan tried to pull
back his hand and had he not been weakened he might
not only have done so, but also heaved Kirk with it.

"He's not dead," Kirk repeated through gritted teeth.

Spock gulped, and as instantly as he'd awakened,
his grip relaxed and his hand fell away. Just as quickly,
his visage returned to its normal, impassive expression.

"Of course not, Captain," he said as he leaned back

in the oddest mixture of a relaxed and yet stiff posture.

The captain's shared look with McCoy didn't answer the question both were likely asking: Was this Spock? The real Spock?

"My apologies, Doctor," the Vulcan said in a cool, normal tone. "Did I injure you?"

"I'll be fine, Spock," McCoy said, studying the man's face intently.

With an accepting nod, Spock then looked to the captain. "My apologies to you as well. I should like to file a full report, explaining my actions—"

"Later, Mister Spock," McCoy interrupted, and when Kirk opened his mouth to speak, the doctor cut him off as well. "I said *later*. He's not eaten in three days and there's only so much intravenous nutrition can do."

Kirk had too many questions and McCoy's lack of curiosity, and insistence that they go unanswered, irritated him to no end. But he nodded anyway.

"Doctor, I assure you—"

"Don't bother, Mister Spock. Bed rest is the prescription, and I intend to see it is filled."

Spock leveled a raised brow, and Kirk might have chuckled his delight at seeing it, if he truly felt the entire episode was over. Something in his gut told him it wasn't.

What of Berlis? He glanced sideways at the troublesome mind just two meters from Spock. Could they keep him in stasis forever? Was it right to do so? And should he someday awaken, what would that do to Spock?

"I'd like him to rest in his quarters," Kirk told McCoy.

"Jim, I don't—"

"This isn't negotiable, Doctor," Kirk hammered. He wanted Spock as far away from Berlis as possible. "I don't want them in the same room. If I could put one in a shuttle, tethered behind the ship, I would."

"I think Mister Spock has gone through his shuttle allotment this month," McCoy jibed lightly. Kirk didn't react to the levity, and neither did Spock. The doctor pressed on. "Fine. So long as he rests, I don't care where." He looked at Spock. "But I intend to check on you hourly."

Lowering his head in assent, Spock agreed.

Once in his cabin, he did not need sleep, yet hourly the doctor insisted he should. The logic of frequent visits and yet expecting one's patient to sleep eluded him.

For Spock, meditation was more required than was slumber, and had McCoy been better versed in Vulcan physiology, he might have understood. There was, of course, a time when Spock had explained it to the doctor, but the rote response was an admonishment to remember his human half.

As if he could forget.

Fingers woven together and steepled at his chin, Spock cleared his mind and concentrated on each singular event since his last meditation, in order, from then until now. Each moment had its own analysis, first in a contextual vacuum, then within the context of the time it occurred, and finally within the greater milieu of every other moment of his life. This was the Vulcan way, the way of his forebears, the learned discipline that had helped an entire race transcend chaos: "Using reason as their guide."

And yet this time nothing felt—not felt—*was* resolved. Hour after hour, between the doctor's quaint interruptions, Spock resolved to begin again and sort happenstance from emotion. Hour after hour, he seemed unequal to the task.

Frustration tensed his muscles and his clasped hands trembled under the strain. The door chimed again, another hour had obviously passed. He closed his eyes, willed his hands to calm themselves, and lowered them to his lap where they were hidden by the desk.

"Enter."

The door opened and McCoy stepped in. "Jim wanted to stop by but I thought you'd rather not be disturbed just yet."

"How singularly astute of you, Doctor."

From McCoy's expression, the intention of Spock's comment was not lost on him.

"Right," he said. "I'll let the computers warn me if

your vitals change drastically and check in on you in the morning."

Spock nodded once, noncommittally.

"And get some sleep," McCoy said as the door closed behind him. "Doctor's orders."

"Indeed," Spock murmured to himself, and returned to his meditation.

Oblivion was damp without the moisture, and freezing yet not cold. The darkness was not a lack of light but a texture unto itself and it extended forever—a vast expanse and yet confining like a hard cocoon. The more he reached out into the void, the tighter it coalesced around him. Worst of all, it was built of the loneliness that even gods refused to touch.

This was Berlis's universe, and the unending pain pressed down on his every atom. Drifting, he called out for the one savior he knew might answer him.

Spock!

The wail blazed on every nerve ending. Spock gasped in psychological pain and physically stumbled. He struggled to keep himself off the deck as Berlis's plaintive cry raked across him. Unprotected and unready for the emotional inundation, what scant order had come from the last twenty hours of work disintegrated in a fraction of a second.

From his bottomless pit of solitude, Berlis clutched

onto the one mind close enough to touch. Spock expected the pleading for companionship Berlis begged for on Home Zero, but in his seclusion the troublesome mind could not truly communicate anymore. All he could do was reach out in misery, which he broadcast in wave after crashing wave.

Spock understood his pain, though he could not have comprehended its extent until Berlis insisted he do so.

In that eternal moment, the Vulcan pretense of sequestering emotion seemed both ceaselessly naïve, and heartrendingly unattainable.

He could bear the tsunami of emotion no longer. It must end.

It must.

Spock prepared himself as quickly as possible, struggling against Berlis's assault. The pain wrenched him. He wrestled against it to gather enough composure to leave his cabin. He traversed relatively unnoticed down the corridors, but once he was alone in the turbolift he couldn't help but allow a terrible sob. He slumped against the wall and with his free hand pounded on his own leg as hard as he could manage without knocking himself down. "Control," he growled through his tightened jaw. "Control!"

The unending tide of despair both pushed the Vulcan away, and pulled him deeper in toward the center of the storm. *There must be relief. There must be.*

Once in sickbay, a nurse called out to him. When

Spock didn't reply, he was certain she went to a comm to contact the doctor.

No matter. He must be free of the unending, heavy, horrific passions.

Berlis lay unnecessarily restrained, his delicate limbs pinned with strips of cloth to the bio-bed. The white aura of energy that enveloped his skull could not end either man's agony.

"Spock!" McCoy's voice.

He did not turn to meet the doctor's face, but heard a click and McCoy spoke again. "Jim, get down here. Now!"

Hesitation would mean suffering without end. Vacillation would hasten the wrong kind of oblivion. The unwanted meld, the unasked-for agony, the unrequited escape . . . logic demanded a distinct path. Morality insisted as well. Judgment wavered when it should not have: *that* was the weakness of the emotional, the illogic that so desperately needed to be purged from the mind.

Boots skidding on the deck must surely have been Kirk's.

Time was short.

Shakily, his arm extended and his hand squeezed closed.

The whine filled their ears as loudly as the wails filled their minds.

And then both went silent.

EPILOGUE

"How is he?" Kirk rolled the phaser over and over in his hand, studying it because he didn't want to look at Spock.

The doctor handed his scanner to the nurse and left Spock on the bio-bed, quietly resting. He motioned Kirk out into his office.

"What's wrong?" Kirk asked, a rock of tension weighing down his stomach.

"What's right?" McCoy said somberly. "Unofficially he's fine."

"Unofficially?" Kirk huffed out in frustration. "Bones—"

"Unofficial because if I put in the record that he's mentally and physically unfit, his career will be ruined."

He crooked a thumb over his shoulder. "You were here. You saw what happened. He murdered Berlis in cold blood."

Kirk gripped the phaser hard. "I saw it. The question is why. Spock's not a murderer." He pointed at McCoy with his free hand. "You know that."

"And I know what I saw. Sure, he's been under great strain—"

"Then write that in your report."

"I will, Jim. But right now—as of this moment—he checks out." McCoy cast his gaze down and shook his head. "I examined him just after, and . . ."

"We have to dig deeper and find out why."

Pivoting on a heel, Kirk marched into sickbay. McCoy followed.

"That'll be all," Kirk told the nurse, and she looked to the doctor for confirmation.

With a slight nod, McCoy hastened her out.

Once the door had closed behind her, Kirk approached one side of Spock's bed and McCoy the other.

Eyes closed, the Vulcan was serene, eyes moving beneath their lids. Was he dreaming? What did he dream about? What did anyone dream about when life was a nightmare?

"Spock."

If he was in a deep sleep, it took little to wake him, for Kirk's call was not loud.

"Captain." He sat up in bed, first on his elbow, then pulling himself into a reclined sitting position. "Doctor," he greeted, but Kirk noticed he would not meet their eyes for more than a split second. And the tone of his voice was not robust. Fatigue didn't seem like the reason. Depression? Confusion?

"Can you talk about what happened?" McCoy asked. He and Spock had numerous disagreements over the years, sharing many harsh words—especially on the doctor's part. But now the warmth he expressed to Spock was almost jarring, as if Spock had been diagnosed with a terminal illness and McCoy felt the need to repent for all his snide remarks at the Vulcan's expense.

"I don't know," Spock said, and Kirk felt his lips part in shock. The man he knew as a pillar of strength and certitude might say something was unknown, or he might admit he lacked enough data for a conclusion, but rarely did he utter "I don't know." Especially when answering a yes-or-no question.

"Spock—" Kirk couldn't demand an answer, though he wanted to. More than wanting to insist on one, he wanted one to simply exist. If Spock truly didn't know . . . "Tell us what you do know," Kirk said.

After a long pause, Spock finally made eye contact that lasted more than a second. "I killed Berlis." It wasn't spoken in his usual impassionate Vulcan timbre, but instead came weakly from barely parted lips.

Kirk and McCoy waited what seemed an eternity for Spock to speak again and offer some explanation.

Finally, the captain prodded him. "Why?"

Preparing with a long sigh, Spock began slowly. "Believing Berlis to be unable to reestablish the mind-meld while in the cortical status field, I lowered the mental disciplines that would block his advances." His voice was less shaky, but still not quite sturdy. "He apparently managed to overcome the confines of the mental suppression—"

"I'm sorry, Spock," McCoy said softly. "I had no idea he'd be able to do that. We should have monitored him more closely."

Spock couldn't bring himself to look at the doctor, but inclined his head in gracious acknowledgment. "No apology is necessary. The Isitri mind is far more complex than most encountered by Federation science."

McCoy said nothing, but exchanged an apologetic glance with Kirk anyway.

Meeting the captain's eyes again, Spock drew in a long, steadying breath and continued. "The nature of a Vulcan mind-meld is dissimilar to the kind of telepathy the Isitri use to communicate. They share thoughts, feelings, dreams . . . and in the case of Berlis—and Meshu—they distribute their will, and their whims." Suddenly he looked just past Kirk, his focus drifting, his lips parting silently for an awkward moment. "Vulcan telepathy is less reflexive and more dynamic. Two minds once melded act as one. One can be more dominant, but it is against the character of the Vulcan mind." He looked up at Kirk again. "One of the many ways in which Isitri and Vulcan telepathy are disparate."

None of this yet spoke to what happened, other than that Berlis had entered Spock's mind against his will. Or was Spock saying that once he did, Berlis wasn't himself, and neither was Spock, but they were a Spock-Berlis hybrid?

Kirk let out a discouraged breath. "What're you saying, Spock? That had you stayed melded with Berlis you could have kept him from overwhelming his own people? Or eventually yours?"

Shaking his head, Spock closed his eyes a moment, seeming to search for the best way to explain his meaning. Kirk couldn't remember having ever seen him do that before.

"No," the Vulcan said finally, and perhaps he was deciding if what Kirk suggested was possible. "By his nature Berlis was what he was. His fate was cast by his immutable nature—"

"Are you saying you killed him because it was his fate to die?" McCoy's tone was partly outraged and Kirk cast him an irritated look. Now wasn't the time.

"Hear him out, Doctor," he ordered. "I want to hear his explanation."

Spock swallowed and shook his head rather sadly. "I have no logical explanation."

By now nothing shocked Kirk any longer, but this statement was more chilling than watching Spock kill an unarmed man.

Except . . . he wasn't unarmed, Kirk remembered.

"He attacked you," Kirk said, writing the report in his head. "And you acted in self-defense."

"He melded with me," Spock said, "and I was not prepared. In his action, he changed me into a part of himself, and I a part of him."

"Spock, did Berlis ask you to . . . did he *want* to die?" Kirk asked, and realized the phaser was crunched in his palm.

"I can't say for certain." The Vulcan met Kirk's gaze with such raw emotion behind his eyes that the hair on the back of the captain's neck stood on end. "Either he wanted to die to end his suffering . . . or I wanted him to die to end mine." Spock shakily sighed and continued, unsteady. "For Berlis, the lack of mental connection was untenable loneliness. As if you or I were to be blinded, deafened, made quadriplegic, and numb to tactile stimulus." He looked from one man to the other. "How long would any of us survive that? Berlis could not endure it. And in reaching out to me, neither could I." He looked past McCoy to Berlis's now empty bed. "I truly don't know if he suggested his ending to me, or I to him." McCoy's brow furrowed and Spock drew the doctor in with the same emotional glance that he'd leveled at Kirk. "Two minds became one, such is the nature of Vulcan telepathy." He looked at the captain again. "And one man's will had become another's, such is the nature of Berlis's troublesome mind. He turns all minds he touches troublesome."

"You're not responsible, Spock," Kirk decided. "Berlis attacked you, made you the instrument of his death." That was the way he wanted it to be.

"Or," Spock said, "we decided that to end our suffering, he needed to die."

"You can't know that." Kirk's jaw was tight. Anger welled within him: at Berlis for his very nature, and at himself for moving Spock down this impossible path. "*He* made the decision: and forced it on you."

"Or," Spock said, heartrending grief streaking his voice, "*I* made the decision, Jim . . . and forced it on him."

"You'll never know," McCoy murmured, his voice thick.

"No," Spock said. "I never shall."

ACKNOWLEDGMENTS

It will come as no surprise to many after reading this book that I have some familiarity with American Sign Language. In fact, as an employee of Gallaudet University (the first higher educational institution for the Deaf and Hard of Hearing in the world), I work with more Deaf people than I do with those who can hear. Generally speaking, I probably sign more than I speak on any given day.

One of my goals with this story was to convey the intricacy of a gestural language, and I hope I accomplished it. Many people have certain misconceptions about sign language, among them the idea that sign is just a series of made-up hand movements meant to represent a spoken tongue. It is not—sign is its own robust language. Any of them that exist—French SL, British SL, Japanese SL, Irish SL, Spanish SL, and so on—has its own syntax, its own etymology, and, for me, its own beauty.

I was careful not to base any Isitri signs on any of the

ASL that I know, but certainly the expressiveness and fondness for my second language was my inspiration for making the Isitri signers, and some of them deaf.

That leads me to the first and most important acknowledgment: my brother Josh (who is a teacher by profession) taught me to sign and so, for giving me a reason to learn and making it easy for me to do so, I am forever in his debt. Because of my learning ASL, I am immersed daily in a culture I enjoy and work with people I like and respect. Hell of a gift, that. Thanks, bro.

Thanks also to Marco Palmieri, who is probably the most flexible and tolerant editor on the planet. It's either my good fortune that it is his nature, or I have pleased the great editing gods. Either way, I wouldn't trade him for the world.

As usual, I have to thank my friends and family for cutting me slack while I moved across the country and worked to finish this book as I began a new job and a new life. It's been a busy summer.

I also want to thank James Cawley and the cast and crew of *Star Trek New Voyages: Phase II*. Not only have they brought me into their fold as one of their extended family, but their graciousness and love of *Trek* has also been a blast. There's nothing quite like being welcomed aboard the *Enterprise* as it looked for William Shatner and Leonard Nimoy forty years ago. Just walking across James's bridge and sitting in *that* chair was inspiration for a hundred *Trek* novels. Basking in the glow of these folks' *Trek* enthusiasm is inspiration for a hundred more. I've made many new and wonderful friends from James's introductions (not least of all him), and while I can't mention them all here, I hope they know this acknowledgment is for each of them, individually and collectively.